CW00869291

The Panther Tales Trilogy

The Queen and the Powerful Pendant

Daniella Rushton

Printed in the United States of America

The Queen and the Powerful Pendant: The Panther Tales Trilogy / Rushton-
1stEdition

ISBN: 978-1-953610-33-1

1.Title. 2. Christian Fantasy. 3. Fantasy. 4. Fiction.
5. Rushton.

Cover illustration art by Jane Mitchell
Fantasy map art by Jane Mitchell
Cover panther art by Zoe Potter

NFB Publishing/Amelia Press
119 Dorchester Road
Buffalo, New York 14213

For more information visit Nfbpublishing.com

Dedicated to my Mother,
and Mary, Mother of God.

'Making the Impossible Possible'

Luke.1 Verses 26 to 38

[26] In the sixth month the angel Gabriel was sent from God to a city of Galilee named Nazareth,
[27] to a virgin betrothed to a man whose name was Joseph, of the house of David; and the virgin's name was Mary.
[28] And he came to her and said, "Hail, O favored one, the Lord is with you!"
[29] But she was greatly troubled at the saying, and considered in her mind what sort of greeting this might be.
[30] And the angel said to her, "Do not be afraid, Mary, for you have found favor with God.
[31] And behold, you will conceive in your womb and bear a son, and you shall call his name Jesus.
[32] He will be great, and will be called the Son of the Most High;
and the Lord God will give to him the throne of his father David,
[33] and he will reign over the house of Jacob for ever;
and of his kingdom there will be no end."
[34] And Mary said to the angel, "How shall this be, since I have no husband?"
[35] And the angel said to her, "The Holy Spirit will come upon you,
and the power of the Most High will overshadow you; therefore the child to be born will be called holy, the Son of God.
[36] And behold, your kinswoman Elizabeth in her old age has also conceived a son; and this is the sixth month with her who was called barren.
[37] For with God nothing will be impossible."
[38] And Mary said, "Behold, I am the handmaid of the Lord; let it be to me according to your word." And the angel departed from her.

The Panther Tales Trilogy

The Queen and The Powerful Pendant

Quotes & Music to accompany your Panther Tales experience.
- Daniella

'Dig deep to keep Believing'

'Only if you Believe, can you make the Impossible Possible'

'Shines upon those that Shine'

'Armour of Light'

'True friends walk alongside us, even when they are not visibly there'

'The way of The Star is to Shine and Serve'

'For some it can take a lifetime. Some, never find the answer'

'Be careful of what you allow into your mind'

'Only if she believed with her full heart could her imagination come to life'

'For where there is good there is always evil'

'Troubles will carve your inner star to shine bright'

'Nail yourself to your Belief'

'Nail yourself to believe Better'

'Every day is a day of light'

'Eyes, mind, heart, wide open'

'The Bridge of Stars'

And many more... read on...

Recommended Music for 'The Queen and the Powerful Pendant'

Beethoven. Symphony No.7. Major Op 92
By Ludwig Van Beethoven.

'Listen and Listen Loud.' – Daniella

This story can be read by itself but is also a sequel to '*The Watchers and The Gifted Ones*' where Hannah befriends a panther, whilst discovering she possesses an extraordinary imaginative gift.

Dark forces are waiting and watching to destroy her happiness.

All she needs to do is to believe in herself and a panther called Parky.

CONTENTS

CHAPTER ONE: MERMAID IN THE GARDEN **15**

CHAPTER TWO: VIRUS OF THE MIND **33**

CHAPTER THREE: ROSE TINTED SPECTACLES **45**

CHAPTER FOUR: PANTHER FAIRIES **55**

CHAPTER FIVE: THE BELIEF COUNCIL **65**

CHAPTER SIX: A ROYAL PALM **79**

CHAPTER SEVEN

PART ONE: A SERIES OF COMPLICATIONS **91**

PART TWO: A SLIPPERY PATH **97**

'THE WATCHERS AND THE GIFTED ONES OF ASHBY BY SEA' FANTASY MAP **112**

CHAPTER EIGHT:

PART ONE: A RECORD OF WRONGDOINGS 114

PART TWO: WHERE THE CROW FLIES 122

CHAPTER NINE: GATHERING IN WINGS OF LOVE 133

CHAPTER TEN: CHRISTMAS CLARITY 141

CHAPTER ELEVEN: THE MAGIC OF MATRIARCHS 151

CHAPTER TWELVE: JIGSAW COTTAGE 160

CHAPTER THIRTEEN: SAVING SOULS 169

CHAPTER FOURTEEN:

PART ONE: PANTHER AT THE OPERA 178

PART TWO: BELIEVE ON CHRISTMAS EVE 184

CHAPTER FIFTEEN:

PART ONE: WATCHERS WATER ASSAULT 191

PART TWO: THE SUPPER BATTLE 205

Chapter One

Mermaid in the Garden

The moon shone brightly upon the heavily studded townhouse door, giving its black exterior a liquid appearance. Hannah had been anxious about arriving home and The Watchers were waiting. Stepping gingerly onto the stone doorstep of the family Georgian townhouse in the small English market town of Ashby by the Sea, she paused. The end of summer was fast approaching, and a refreshing early evening chill had long squashed the remnants of the days sun.

Turning and tilting her head back towards the street she sniffed the earthy, musty evening air. There was a distinct smell of algae. Unaware of it before, she casually raised her eyebrows, pushed open the front door, and shrugged it off. Stepping inside, she once again found herself standing upon a highly polished black and white tiled hall floor.

Outside, the numerous waterways, which occupied the town, mainly consisting of brooks and streams, were bubbling away with new activity. Long ago, a new breed of Watcher had formed here, different in appearance, but with the same characteristics. News had reached the dark underground that the favoured Gifted One had returned. For centuries the small market town and surrounding villages had been a strong foothold for the preying cult called The Watchers and their evil curse.

It was quite extraordinary how the cuckoo clock hanging in the dining room, left of the hall, chimed at the exact moment she had walked through the front door. The familiar little people in their traditional German dress waltzed out of their alpine hut as a kind of 'welcome home' serenade. It comforted her feeling of unease, if only momentarily.

Hannah felt different, changed.

Straightforward and like her father; a logical thinker, nothing ever really ruffled her feathers. This combined with her artistic flare gave her a relaxed demeanour. Her life had changed in every possible way, up until this very moment. Even with its challenges, she had felt in full of acceptance of it.

Now, confronting her family felt overwhelming. Like her mother in some ways, she liked things just so. Thrown into the mix was the unknown situation of Amelia, her sister, creating an anxiety that made her heart heavy. There were rumbles between them just before she had left for America, as there had been for some time. Except on that day, Amelia held a look in her eye she had never seen before. At the time and surprisingly, she hadn't given it another thought. After discovering she was Gifted whilst at Mini's, she had reflected upon it. Now she felt it was a look she kind of understood and recognised; a look from time to time she would see, over and over again.

Hannah was a Gifted One. A gift of imaginary power, granted by The Great Star of the Cosmos.

She lived in a world of The Watchers and The Gifted Ones, where everyone is born with the potential to receive The Gift. Thus, leaving the unaware souls called Naturals free of imaginary power. The good versus evil forces which dwelt among them were forces beyond their recognition. Naturals lived blissfully unaware, with the only fear slightly gripping such locals being the rumours that perpetuated around the castle, and these were generally spoken about in jest.

The Watchers were equally Gifted but having lost faith and belief in their Gift from the Star, their power was controlled shrouded in darkness. They took perverse pleasure in transforming themselves and observing and spying on the Gifted Ones, in the hope of putting an end to their extraordinary power and their Mindful joy.

Before the summer, Hannah didn't know she possessed such a gift. She now realised her mother had known all along because her grandmother, Mini, had told her. There was a slight sense of anger that gripped her at not being told sooner. She was wondering if Amelia was Gifted as well and what did she know? Aside from the fact she bickered with her twin, it was part of the reason her parents had sent her to Palms in America. A place the family would often say was oceans away, where Mini lived and where Hannah's mother knew she would discover her gift. On the day she had left her hometown, Amelia seemed bruised and brittle, clearly annoyed at being left behind. At the time it seemed an illogical step to separate the pair, although their differences as they aged had become more apparent. As little ones they played endlessly with eyes that didn't judge. It was with this in mind the day Hannah left, that she saw her surroundings differently. True, the historic market town with its independently owned shops, cobbled main street and interesting architecture charmingly stood, as it always had, like a giant Aladdin's cave. But on that day, it provoked endless memories for her, such as the sisters playing in the street alley ways, paddling in the brooks, popping into the many individual stores, chatting like family to the owners. On reflection, it had been heartless to split them and the 'unknown' about Amelia seemed even crueller, but it was all part and parcel of The Great Star's plan.

"Hi, I'm home!" she yelled cautiously extending her neck, to enable her voice to reverberate down the long thin hall, where she could see a pair of pink stylish sneakers sitting neatly up against the hall kickboard. They were of course Amelia's, who, by all accounts from her mother, was in trouble and the cause of Hannah's hasty return home. Seeing the sneakers briefly warmed her heart, making her want to kick her own battered pair off and line them up alongside Amelia's well-presented pair. They were *so* different, she thought. How would their relationship be now she was Gifted?

No one appeared and not a sound other than the various clocks ticking could be heard. In the absence of any family, she glanced into the huge antique mirror which dominated the right-hand wall of the hall. Each of its four edges was heavily gilded in gold, with overhanging ornate carvings. In the corner of her eye whilst blearily looking at herself, she caught sight of the portrait of Mini and Hunter, her grandparents. In it, Mini was pregnant with her mother Belinda. She sighed, recalling how only twenty-four hours ago, her grandmother, now oceans away in America, had been telling her about her grandfather's demise at Ashby castle, allegedly at the hands of The Watchers.

Looking now at the portrait she could see the worry in Hunter's pale blue eyes, behind his signature thick black glasses. Her mind drifted in amazement at the realisation that Mini had not really changed in her appearance from the portrait, some forty years ago. She seemed eternally youthful, an exceptional woman on so many levels. Hannah now understood it was Mini's profound trust in her Gift from The Great Star that perpetuated her glowing aura.

She wondered, now being a Gifted One, if the Timms home would emanate the same enchantment and warmth that Mini's did. After all Mini, also a Gifted One, had lived and raised her daughter Belinda here, before moving back to America.

The portrait evoked surreal memories of her extraordinary summer with Mini. Combined with travel fatigue, it left her in a daze staring into the mirror. The gilded edging, seemed to protrude out from the looking glass, closing in on her. It felt surreal and the need to fall asleep whilst standing began to consume her weary limbs. With it came a desire to walk straight through the house into the garden in search of what she didn't know, probably in search of family. This subconscious zest for the outdoors woke her as she began ruffling her hands through her long straight blonde hair which hung limp, framing her tiny, freckled face.

It was certainly odd that no one was home, Belinda amongst many things, upheld these finer traditions and so it was customary to be greeted in the Timms family hall, or so her mother believed it to be.

Hannah's patient and tired blue eyes wandered back to the reflection of her pendant in the mirror of a porcelain panther, the colour of copper. A present from her grandmother at the end of the summer, it glowed in the now moonlight, which had begun to break through the stained-glass window above the front door.

'Parky', she fondly whispered, resting her delicate fingers upon the panther pendant, as she recalled the life-sized statue of him, frozen in time upon a shelf in her grandmother's home. Now, with her extraordinarily new Gifted power and recent miraculous events, he was alive beyond imaginary power and his spirit lived on.

Tossing her backpack onto the floor in her typically scruffy fashion, the whirring sound of Joy, the family's Artificial Intelligence (AI) coming from the end of the hall near the kitchen broke the silence.

"Hello Hannah, you are home." She said in her unmistakable melodic, robotic tones. Devised and built in the shape of a human-being by Hannah's father, Timothy, the family scientist, Joy robotically manoeuvred herself over towards Hannah. Named by Belinda, because she did exactly that, bring Joy to the family. She would often accompany Belinda in many of her activities, such as her interest in art, which she had inherited from her own grandfather William Cernobbio, whom sadly she had never meet.

Joy also added a mindful balance to the family, accepting all things different and with that understanding, as with technology, recognizing things constantly change. This seemed to lighten Belinda's feeling of immense responsibility, nurturing the twins Gifted power. One, which Mini her mother had dutifully stepped in to help her with, when she herself had sensed from correspondence that the twins were growing quite differently, and that they may benefit from learning their newfound powers whilst having time apart. Being a twin herself, Mini understood the profound differences between the girls. Hannah had inherited this sense of honourability and took her newfound Gifted power like her mother and grandmother, seriously.

Joy's body shape was that of a female human, dressed simply in t shirt and jeans. Within the mechanics of her body lay lights and written in her code the ability to respond to human recognition and interaction. Today, upon seeing Hannah, who Joy recognised as a family member, tiny lights on her chest area flashed in the shape of pink and red hearts. Both her and Amelia were fond of Joy, the elder sister they never had. Seeing Joy today, she became aware for the first time of her uncomplicated, simple approach to the world. She rather envied that she was devoid of any complicated emotion.

She was a tall AI with thick black long hair. Belinda would usually tie it back, but both girls loved playing with it, creating all kind of wacky styles, something they did together. Hannah had missed it she thought and recalled how Amelia would often say that her father had designed their very own Amazonian princess.

She also marvelled, like her father at the science behind it. It was quite something that Joy could be switched on and off and plugged in, to recharge like an electric car. Before the summer she learned that her father was working on a free charging system that meant Joy could be active whilst still charging. He was always bettering her in some way or other.

Hannah noticed the similarity of Joy's vulnerability to that of her imaginary friend from her grandmother's home, 'Nancy the lamp'. A tall floor lamp with the body of a Greek goddess and a liberty torch held up in her right hand. Sadly, due to the Mindful Watchers she no longer existed. She shuddered, tightly shutting her eyes as her mind drifted once again to The Watchers. It seemed; she was more in tune with her emotions since she had become Mindfully Gifted.

A power unlike any other. Hannah's imagination could now stir incredible energy, enabling whatever she imagined coming to life. The only condition being, *'only if she truly believed it could.'* She quickly reflected upon how the process occurred. Radiating a warmth and glow, her mindful energy would rise, and a huge tunnel of light would appear to beam from the middle of her chest. A bridge to another world.

Her mood lifting, grinning, she was eager to hear her scientist father's explanation behind it all.

The chatter in her mind suddenly started to build and drifted back to her grandmother's home and Belinda the portrait, another imaginary friend. A beautiful blonde-haired lady dressed in a green sweater with long red nails, who lived in the frame of one of Mini's bedroom pictures above a fireplace. Previously, from time-to-time Hannah had thought she resembled her own mother, even from when she spoke, down to her husky tones. It had since been revealed that Belinda the portrait, her imaginary friend was a painting of her mother!

After carefully listening and being guided by The Great Star of The Cosmos, Belinda's gift had enabled her to communicate through the portrait with Hannah, granting her a much-needed part in the nurturing of Hannah's special Gift.

Recalling her mother's face, revealed in the portrait against the backdrop of a castle in chaos like the one in Ashby by the Sea, Belinda had foretold that all was not well at home and that Amelia was in trouble. It had worried her, perpetuating the anxiety she now felt, wondering if the trouble she was in, was any direct relation to The Watchers? Amelia hadn't ever got herself in trouble, in any real sense. She was so well received at school; only once had she been falsely accused of stealing some 'old money' that had been on display in an exhibition at school. It was later found out two well-known gossipy girls from their school had 'set her up' by placing the coins in her pocket. If anything, it would be her own tomboy curiosity that would have caused the family any kind of upset. She began to wonder, yet again, what had gone on whilst she was away. Before leaving America, Mini had proceeded to both warn and share all she knew, in what would become Hannah's continued quest against The Watchers. Details such as her grandfather's connection with the leader of The Spectacle Council of Watchers, Victor, and his enthrallment with the dark world he shared with The Great Gifted Nickolous. Then there were the deadly species of Flying Watcherfish, different to The Watchers at Mini's who transformed into crows. These winged creatures, about the size of a bird, had the body of a lizard and the face and beak of a crow. She hadn't imparted any information about Amelia though.

Mini had tried to explain that the new breed was like the Watchercrows of her hometown, who transformed their imaginary power into their alter egos, crows, to prey upon and watch The Gifted. These new slippery stalkers seemed nightmarish.

"Joy, where is everyone?"

Still feeling confused as well as a bit abandoned, with a genuine concern in the absence of family, Hannah, as most people tend to do upon arriving home, made her way towards the kitchen to make a cup of tea. Joy followed, processing her question. For a moment, the feeling of happiness that is usually associated with homecoming, flooded back. The smell of her mother's perfume lingered in the air; favourite cups lay abandoned on the counter tops. She could even see one of Amelia's hair bands lying dormant with thick red strands of hair sticking out of it, resembling some spidery creature.

It was a traditional townhouse kitchen, a fire at one end accompanied by a cosy seating arrangement and a large cooker at the other, offering eternal warmth. The kitchen played a major part in the Timms household. The pile of magazines and newspapers on the floor by the couches and chairs stood like mini skyscrapers, precariously managing their dizzying heights, whilst possessively holding on to the dust. Everyone was responsible for contributing to the running of the house, with Belinda as captain. However, on orders by Timothy, no-one could dust or clean around his pile of papers as he was, 'still reading some editions,' and knew exactly the order they were in.

The austere white wall tiles were reminiscent of Harrison's, the butcher's meat store on the High Street, countless cooking utensils strategically hung upon them. Copper pans hung like oversized windchimes from the ceiling's black beams. The kitchen was in part kept orderly. Belinda ran a tight ship at home and the large, oval shaped wooden table with its six matching chairs was the hub of it. Peeling a chair away before slumping into it, Hannah recalled the wide range of emotions this huge wooden beast had provoked. From the laughter to the bickering to deep meaningful discussions and rousing arguments, all had taken place here.

She glanced up the same stag's head which had hung in the same place for what seemed like an eternity, it stared piercingly back, gripping the wall it was mounted to. Just like her grandmother's, oddities filled their home and for Hannah, in her mind, her family history was beginning to fall into place.

"Belinda, Tim and Amelia are out of the house Hannah, you must not worry, back soon."

Joy eventually replied, perhaps from an inbuilt recorded message. She neatly presented Hannah with a cup of tea. Like nearly all AI's she spoke in a direct, matter-of-fact way.

Caressing the mug with both hands, Hannah breathed in deeply, in through her nostrils then out, closing her eyes. She had seen her mother do it, it was a snap meditation or something. What was going on? She thought. She still had a desire to go into the garden…When she opened her eyes, Joy was bent over in front of her, leaning in, staring directly at her panther pendant. Tilting her head down to see what she was looking at, to her surprise the pendant was glowing, gently pulsating on her T-shirt. The pace at which it pulsed quickened, and an unknown force that felt strangely familiar drew Hannah to her feet and without realising it, her desire to go outside was realised as she drifted towards the back door which led into the garden.

The rather large walled garden had an elevated area, reached by four brick steps directly in the middle. At either side, at the top of the steps sat two impressive statues, to the right, one of a Queen and to the left a King.

Iron railings sat upon a wall of large stones, neatly dividing the upper from the lower part of the garden, which the family called the yard. Scruffy style pots filled with either failed planting or out of season shrubs dangling over, lined the walls.

Living in a 'damp old town', as her father called it, had given to years of crumbling render on the walls, revealing ghostly damp patches despite ongoing maintenance, but these were in part disguised by three large art boards, collected by Belinda from the local charity she served on Ashby Arts Festival. A huge Victorian style streetlamp stood in the corner illuminating the boards.

The upper part of the garden was formal with a small central ornamental pond. Surrounding it were a dozen or so small finely manicured topiary trees and to walk among them, one felt like a giant in a garden maze. It was just one of the games the girls played together when they were younger. They would imagine as they walked up the steps, the King and Queen either side, sprinkling magic dust over them, instantly making them grow as tall as the tallest of giants. Pretending miniature people lived in the garden below, they would divide the trees amongst each other and with the Queen and King overlooking become gigantic princesses in a pretend kingdom.

Hannah found herself stood at the bottom of the steps in the still pure moonlight, peering slightly up towards the statue of the Queen. 'Queen Nail.' The name she herself as a little girl had given to it, when her jovial father had announced one day, 'I have a Queen for the garden!'

Running up to the statue, she had been about six years old at the time and meeting it head height, Hannah had spontaneously thrown her arms around it thinking this was her chance to hug a real Queen. The statue toppled and pulling away, but not quickly enough, it fell headfirst onto her tiny foot; the crown of the statue breaking her right-hand big toe and nail. Hence the statue was named, Queen Nail.

Standing around 3-foot-tall, Queen Nail had a gentle gracious face. Robed in a belted long dress and tunic, a veil securely kept in place by a simple yet majestic medieval crown. It was not hard for the girls to imagine her as a real Queen in a costume of silk materials, textures of velvet in bold colours, along with the gemstones that would have adorned her crown.

The panther pendent continued to pulsate as Hannah stared at the Queen. Above, in the moon lit sky, a star shone brightly. It was The Great Star the of Cosmos. The progenitor of the universe.

It was all knowing and her salvation from the evil Watchers when she was at her grandmothers. Its long, narrow rays seemed to almost touch the garden wall. The middle of the star, just like her panther pendant, appeared to pulsate. In that moment, her imagination, for the first time since being at home, began to come alive. The same familiar warmth caressed her body as her energy levels began to rise and a huge tunnel of light appeared to beam out from the middle of her chest.

Queen Nail, clothed by the light from the star, shimmered and began an extraordinary transformation. The crown on her head dissolved, replaced by a crown of stars, which floated over her silver hair as it glistened in the moon light. Her tunic shortened, turning a luxurious blue velvet. She then sprouted the tail of fish with scales of blue in every shade imaginable. She had transformed into a mermaid and began to hover mid-air. Her arms extended with her palms open and shafts of light from the great star shone between her fingers, revealing incredibly beautiful long blue nails.

In her imaginative state Hannah was not only speechless but a little apprehensive.

"Hello dear Hannah," she said in a gentle voice. "Do not be afraid."

Queen Nail peered up into the night sky as a constellation appeared in the form of Parky the Panther, courtesy of The Great Star of the Cosmos. It seemed to take up the entire sky, the colour of midnight blue. The stars that formed the head of the panther began to sway and sparkle in the tranquillity of time. They swivelled slowly to look at Hannah, she could see Parky's starry eyes smiling back at her and from the constellation, his meaningful voice offered strict yet loving instructions, in equal measure.

"The Watchers as Mini told you, are in Ashby-by-the Sea. They look different to Watchercrows but are still Watchers. They have been waiting for your return as a favoured Gifted One. Use your power to make friends, to stand upright amid the forthcoming storms. I am with you always. You couldn't wish for a better friend right here..." and whilst looking down towards Queen Nail, the constellation of his stars melted away.

Queen Nail, floating above the ornamental pond in the garden, in her gentle voice, said to Hannah,

"Come," and beckoning her over, said, "what do you see?" her palms faced upwards, and her long nails pointed down towards the pond.

The lily pads wafted to the side of the pond revealing Hannah's reflection, ruins of a medieval castle also appeared. It was the same castle her mother had revealed to her from the portrait, except now she could see it in more detail.

Raised on higher ground, surrounded by a wide ditch of sunken land, resembling a dried-up moat, the ruins of the castle had thick walls made of sandstone. There was a huge great tower at one end with steep tiny steps exposed, once hidden by thick walls. Large empty arched windows hauntingly peered down on the many people, of all ages, seemingly being rounded up.

Forming lines along the castle walls where once one would have probably imagined a great hall or a chapel were what looked like the different kind of Watcher, flying lizards, no larger than a crow.

People were wailing and coughing caused by the dust, from the flapping of these grotesque creatures small prehistoric looking wings, against the stone walls.

Then the castle faded and a wilderness where it had been, began to appear, with several large ponds dotted in and around it. Hannah began to see her reflection once more as the scene of the castle faded completely away.

"Hannah, our hearts are once again a battleground for good and evil, the darkness we learn, lurks everywhere. Now not only Watchercrows but also Flying Watcherfish. But do not fear, I will help you my dear one." Queen Nail smiled gently before being swallowed by the pond, dropping seamlessly in a vertical pencil dive into an unknown underwater world.

The panther pendant left Hannah's body wrapped in warmth from the imaginative experience. Taking it all in, she took a long deep breath. Like so many times during the summer, she was left feeling bewildered. Queen Nail was again stone and statuesque, back on top of the steps.

"So, it's true, there are different kind of Watchers." she whispered to herself, gazing at Queen Nail.

"Yes, there are." replied a sinister voice from somewhere behind her in the yard. The tone of the yes sounded more like a hiss with evil undertones

Hannah froze. She recognised that voice. It sounded like Victor, the leader of the Watchers, who back in the summer had terrorised her on Spyglass Hill Drive, before cowardly fleeing the mindful battle having his wickedness drowned out by the rays of The Great Star of the Cosmos. Yet it sounded shriller. Fearfully, slowly, she turned around, it felt like an eternity.

It was her twin Amelia! Instantly recognisable by the silhouette of her flaming red hair, yet her face, in the moon light, was that of Victor. Pointed and mean with piercing deep set dark eyes, the face grinned wickedly back at her.

Fear wrapped her as she shook her head from side to side, her hair swished across her face and a scream prisoned deep within her, tried to break out.

"Home then?" the voice said sarcastically, except now it was that of Amelia. Her face restored to that which Hannah recognised instantly, a round pretty face with freckles like her own and soft hazel brown eyes.

"Oh, it's you Amelia" she said, relieved as she walked over to her, still feeling shaken. Awkwardly, they embraced. Amelia stiffened as if offended and pulling back, flicked her hair, ever conscious of her image. A tiny smile broke from her face, revealing a slither of happiness to see Hannah return home, but her pride intervened, swivelling she stalked to the back door to the house.

"Where have you been? I've been home a while." Hannah said raising her voice, watching her stalk off.

'Same old Amelia,' she thought. 'Different Ashby-by-the-Sea.' And followed her into the house, looking back over her shoulder to Queen Nail as she went.

So, the spirit of Parky the panther lives on. And I, The Great Star of the Cosmos will continue to guide Hannah in this part of her earth journey and shine upon those that shine. Reminding them of their gifted obligations, in the battle of the Mindful Watchers. Who, we begin to learn, can appear in different disguises.

Follow me now, as I continue to share this tale of courage and belief.

Chapter Two

Virus of the Mind

Victor's face imprinted upon Amelia's was haunting Hannah.

With her new Gifted eyes came an overriding fearful urge to find out what was going on, explore her hometown and find out more about this different form of Watcher. She had never felt alone where she had been raised and lived her entire life. Now home held a hidden enemy making it feel alien. She knew the town like the back of her hand with all its quirkiness there wasn't a place she had not explored with Amelia. When they were younger, 'Toy town' as their father would sometimes jokily name it, resembled at first glance a movie set, with its cobbled streets, period buildings and enchanting alley ways.

At home and reunited, the family seemed unsettled; much was unsaid. Hannah was not alone with the feeling of being 'on edge'.

Hugs had occurred and Belinda, teary with the emotion of Hannah's homecoming amidst other things, had decided to divert her emotional energy into her culinary skills, whilst Tim, with Autumn beckoning lit the first fire of the season.

The atmosphere was tense, like everyone knowing something, but no one saying anything, as much had changed and much was still changing.

There was the smell of freshly lit wood in the burner, met with the aroma of fresh dewy vegetables. Belinda, with nails that were always painted, was peeling and chopping, displaying an array of perfectly sized cut vegetable squares.

Like Mini, her own mother, Belinda was conscious of appearances and a green preppy bow tied back her straight blonde hair, matching her sweater. Tim was a kind, tall, redheaded man, devoted to his scientific calling.

The twin's parents were opposites in almost every way. His scruffiness, countless books and slight 'mad professor style' was counteracted by his loving, calm, jolly attitude.

Hannah decided to head upstairs to her bedroom. The wink she thought she saw, passing Mini's portrait in the hall, she simply put down to tiredness. Mini had a signature wink; that and clapping her hands together formed some of her most endearing characteristics which Hannah fondly recalled.

Running, she flopped onto her bed. It nursed the wall under a huge window of neatly divided glass panes. Quickly, kneeling up to the windowsill, resting her head upon her hands, she peered out, it overlooked the garden. She could see Queen Nail; the moonlight had softened her stone exterior.

Gifted Ones imaginary friends became crystallised in their minds through memories and experiences encountered in life's important, as well as joyful events.

The twins had always shared a bedroom, however just before the summer and with their seventeenth birthdays looming and each needing their own space, it was decided that they would have their own rooms.

One could describe Hannah's bedroom as 'scruffy', with clothes strewn on the floor, posters placed on the walls with sticky tape, crumbled at the edges. Like her father, books and magazines remained mostly scattered. Being a lover of art, some of her own work also adorned the walls. In a relaxed dresser, she did keep her t shirts and sweaters in some order, but her jewellery which consisted mainly of bracelets, piled high upon her wrist, were heaped high on a hand painted dish on her bedside cabinet. Amelia's room, situated at the front of the house, with a view of the castle, always remained neat. Just as her mother Belinda ran the house, Amelia kept her bedroom in an orderly fashion. Among her many achievements, being an allrounder, of course, Amelia was head girl at school. Hannah had never felt one ounce of jealously at her sister being given such an honourable position.

It was particularly important to Amelia that her desk was moved to her new room, and she had decided to put it in front of the window, overlooking the castle. Towards the back of the room, dedicated to her fashion and beauty interests, her hair accessories carefully assembled on long vertical poles erected by Tim. From a distance, they resembled show jumping award paraphernalia, with bows and bands piled high. Her clothes hung in a huge freestanding wardrobe, like the one in the story, 'The Lion, the Witch & the Wardrobe', and were all arranged, hung in colour order, or neatly folded on the internal shelves. Shoes at the bottom were boxed and labelled with only a few random pairs of unboxed sneakers.

Flaming red haired Amelia was focused, sometimes awkward and critical, but had a good heart. Hannah, as we know, was most like her father, taking a more laid-back approach to life than Amelia. She was relaxed in a tom boyish way, yet she possessed similar qualities to that of her twin, being trustworthy and honourable, if not sometimes feisty and valiant when needed.

So, on that early autumnal evening, as the nights were beginning to draw in, and most households beginning to nestle down for the long winter evenings ahead, Amelia was prepping for the start of her final years at school. Whilst Hannah was quite simply taking time to ponder, with her head in her hands and elbows leant upon the windowsill. They had not really conversed since she had arrived home.

Firstly, she thought of Tom her boyfriend, whom she had met at her grandmothers, and who she was very much hoping she would receive a letter from soon. He had promised to correspond regularly and 'somehow make it work to visit her' in England. Remembering him telling her those exact words, warmed her heart. She wondered what he would think of the eccentric town she lived in and could not wait for the day when they would walk the cobbled streets together. She would be able to explain her hometown to him. She knew though that he had much to work out himself and to see how life would progress, following the summer's events. Tom was a Watcher when she had first met him. Together, they had battled his troubled past, mental health, and fought in unison in the Battle of Minds. Tom had gallantly ridden his unicorn, which had been gifted to him for use in the battle, particularly when confronting Victor. Hannah blushed in the warmth of their innocent romance, longing to hear from him, even though it had only been a few days. Then secondly, she thought of Amelia again, in the bedroom next door. That big question lay unanswered. Was Amelia Gifted? And thirdly, why was she in trouble? The unsaid part of their greeting in the kitchen was all tied up in this mystery. The boil, as far as Hannah was concerned, was ready for lancing. She felt unnecessarily suspicious of Amelia and could not understand the increased hostility from her. The other time she had encountered similar feelings was when Tom had betrayed her, and it was then that her own mental health had been tested.

Joy's heavy feet, stomping up the stairs, broke Hannah's thought process. It was of course the knock for dinner which was always summoned in one of two ways. Either by a bell, that Joy rang in the hall if she was helping Belinda prepare, or a knock at the bedroom door.

Both girls upon hearing the familiar heavy feet, met on the stairs. The smell of vegetable pie had reached the house's lofty parts.

"Hey! How's the room? Nice view of the castle!" Hannah said cheerily to her twin. It was a probing question, without thinking about it she had subconsciously made a link between Amelia and the castle. An inner voice whispered,

'What devil daunts the stone walls of not only the castle but of heart and mind?'

"Yep, it's nice," she replied abruptly, before diverting her glance to Hannah's pendant.

Hannah felt the breath of the inner voice pass by her, it made the hairs upon her neck snap straight.

"New necklace?" Amelia remarked in a sarcastic tone, swishing her red mane in front of Hannah before swivelling again and stomping quite heavily, but not quite as Joy did, down the stairs.

"A present from Mini." Hannah said flatly, in the direction of her walking, still affected by the ghostly voice.

Following her dutifully, she passed by Mini's portrait and momentarily felt a warmth generated from the pendant, easing the chill only a minute ago she had experienced.

Dinner at home was always a lively affair. Often, debates would lead to strong spirited speech and Tim would often orchestrate conversation by playing devil's advocate bringing the table to a crescendo then bringing it down a tempo by smoothing things over when conversation would get heated. This evening, the mood was different, not just because of Hannah's homecoming. Something was brewing in the air. Sitting all together, Hannah began to see the resemblance of Mini, in her mother and sister in looks and strength of character.

Amelia having been nurtured through the summer by her mother into becoming a Gifted One, was on the verge of receiving her Gift. However, unseen obstacles had retained doubts. Without true belief, her imagination would not come to life. She wasn't a Natural though, as an awareness had been acknowledged and a presence of The Great Star felt.

Belinda, also Gifted, had been waiting anxiously for Hannah's return and for the right time to talk with both girls about their miraculous powers. Even more so with the recent events surrounding Amelia, she knew more than she was sharing, trusting the process.

Feeling the tension but perplexed in understanding the reason, Tim was a liberal Natural. He fully acknowledged and respected the Great Star theory but edged to believing in science rather than unfathomable power.

"We eat, then we discuss." Tim said jovially, ruffling his hands through his red hair. A habit of his, often when nervous.

Throughout dinner there was plenty of chit chat not only about the summer and the influx of tourists, but also town folk. It was not unusual to dissect the daily goings on of Ashby-by-the-Sea. The sharp intake of tourism, Tim said, had certainly kept the old town busy. He went on, commenting on the number of photos he had seen being taken of the castle. "Watching behind a lens, instead of seeing with their eyes wide open." And chuckled.

His random statement kept Hannah wondering if many of the tourists could have been Watchers, she noticed her mother raise her eyebrows too. But she was not left in peace to reflect, as throughout the meal, she could see Joy staring quite obsessively with a degree of determination, towards her necklace. Belinda noticing this too, tried to divert her attention. Unbeknown to the others, she knew the power of the pendant.

"Joy dear," said Belinda "Talk to me about the book you are reading to me at the moment."

Many a happy hour was spent listening to Joy reading aloud, her audible library was quite impressive now.

As Hannah peered down to the pendant, which by now was quite clearly distracting everybody, she felt its warmth upon her chest. It began to pulsate, and the copper colour of the panther glowed, for some reason she glanced to Amelia who returned her gaze with a sad look.

Then, something unfathomable began to occur. Hannah's eyelids became heavy, tremendously heavy, so much so that she was unable to keep them open. In the background, slightly muffled, she could hear her mother's voice.

"Hannah are you alright darling? Tim, what's wrong with her, help her!" For even Belinda was unaware of this situation.

She could not only hear her mother's husky, well-spoken tones, but could also feel her trembling hand on her forearm, shaking it in concern. She thought she heard Amelia muttering and a chair being drawn away from the table.

"How weird. Wow. Look at the necklace, it's really glowing." She heard Amelia say.

All the time her eyelids felt forcibly pressed down, whilst the warmth of the pendent raised her energy levels.

Like a forced premonition, it all became clear in her mind's eye. The same image of the castle revealed by her mother and more recently Queen Nail, started to appear in the distance, with a young woman walking towards it.

It was Amelia. Her expression was glazed, her arms slightly raised in front, as if she were sleep walking. Like bees around pollen, lizard style creatures with wings flew around her head, leading her to the direction of the castle. They were The Flying Watcher-fish, which Mini, Queen Nail, and Parky had told her about.

As her eyelids began to regain strength, the image dissolved and fluttering, she opened them. Seconds for her felt like an eternity for the family and it was at this point the unfathomable power came over all The Gifted Ones in the kitchen.

Regaining her composure and before anyone said anything, Belinda, Hannah, and Amelia began to demonstrate the power of their imaginations coming to life. As the warmth filled their entire bodies, warming every bone, muscle and vein, huge shafts of light poured from out of their chests. It was reminiscent of three strong beams surging from a coastal lighthouse into the dark depths of the night.

Tim and Joy, unable to see a thing except the pendant glowing in all its splendour, were exempt from such wonders, for now.

The beams of light seemed to stretch beyond the kitchen wall, like the sea stretches towards the horizon. In the far distance appeared the gigantic face of Parky. By revealing his presence to them all simultaneously, hope lay that Amelia may find faith in her own

Gift. At a crucial time, when the darkness had already started to claw its way into her life, she was on the verge of believing.

In his deep and meaningful voice, he repeated the same instruction he had given to Hannah.

"Belinda, Hannah, and dear Amelia," acknowledging all individually and in turn, nodding his head to each. "Amid the forthcoming storm with The Watchers, stand upright, help one another and make friends. Use the power you have been granted."

Fading away, his voice could still be heard as he said, "I am with you always."

Tim sat feeling powerless, seeing all three women in his life looking peaceful, serene, and very much in control of whatever activity was occurring for them. 'This was illogical and flawed science' he thought, ruffling his hands through his hair in fascination. Joy remained fully focused on Hannah's pendent.

Only Gifted Ones could witness one another's imaginary power and now each would be able to see their imaginative friends.

Hannah's Gifted imagination brought forth Queen Nail, the majestic mermaid, hovering mid-air. She looked upon the three women as her crown of stars swayed above her head caused from the motion of her tail fluttering. The different shades of blue, from her tail, flickered as she swayed, turned, and flipped.

Next, Belinda's Gifted imagination ignited. The stags head mounted upon the kitchen wall came to life as a stately four-legged beast. Hannah was not surprised that her mother might befriend the old chap, and for a moment she became distracted by her mother's voice, "Girls! Look! Isn't he magnificent? Meet Cork, my Scottish stag."

Into the gigantic space, his entire body leapt forth, breaking out from the kitchen tiles. His hooves slid as he landed upon the kitchen table. He was huge, magnificent, and standing proud as he snorted, thrusting his powerful chest forward. His antlers, like solid branches of oak, were long, lean, and intimidating.

"He is a reminder of all living creatures, of untamed nature." Belinda declared.

Amelia's doubts about her Gift instantly faded when she saw Parky. Finally, she was a believer as she witnessed her sister and mother's Gifts. The experience was both overwhelming and enchanting. Her Gifted imagination was realised in the form of Joy, the AI, who transformed into an Amazonian princess. In the light of Amelia's imagination, Joy stood up and walked out of her AI state into that of a beautiful Amazonian warrior.

At the same height, she looked formidable, with the same features and long black hair, which seemed longer and silkier. Her simple two-piece garment, a long skirt that flapped in the breeze of her authority, and a bandeau top, were the colour taupe and around each of her upper arms, she wore bracelets, resembling snakes.

"Amelia!" Joy cooed in a high-pitched voice. Hannah felt she recognised her imaginative friend.

"Joy, you really are real now!" Amelia replied innocently. One could see an instant friendship, formed in pure light.

"Hello, I'm Cork." The stag said whilst deeply coughing. First turning to Joy, then to Queen Nail, he knelt on one of his front legs, lowering his antlers in respect.

The kitchen was now a vast space that seemed to stretch into eternity. Full of light and energy.

Just as the imaginative friends were greeting one another, Hannah noticed something flying around Amelia. About the size of a large bumble bee, tiny black Flying Watcher Fish were circling her head, like flying spiders weaving a web. Alarmed, her Gifted energy suddenly shifted, and Queen Nail vanished. Amelia, oblivious to the mindful thieves, sat ensconced in her blissful state.

Noticing Hannah's energy dropping, The Watchers suddenly abandoned their work and looking over at the panther pendent pulsating, disappeared. Amelia was plunged back into reality, fazed and disturbed.

What potent powers did this new Watcher possess, to boldly enter the home and imaginary power of the Gifted Ones?

Could Amelia whilst Gifted be infected by The Watchers? It was like a virus of the mind.

Chapter Three

Rose Tinted Spectacles

The majority of The Gifted Ones in Ashby-by-the-Sea had become infected by The Watchers, including Amelia, meaning the girls would not be returning to school for the Autumn term. Belinda had received a call from Mrs. Gives, the Headmistress at Tower High School, the same evening Amelia discovered her Gift.

"In no uncertain terms can the school open, Belinda. Many of The Gifted Ones, students *and* teachers included, have become infected. Wandering off at all times throughout the day, seemingly, 'sleep walking' to the castle." She spoke in a rather cynical manner.

Pamela was in her sixties and went beyond the role of Headmistress, taking an almost parental role in her duties. Her short stout frame with more than ample bosom complimented her steady, maternal image. Widowed at an early age, one could say she was 'married to the school.' Her unofficial, self-imposed uniform consisted of practical elasticated waist trousers in a variety of colours, with coordinating matching tops. A string of pearls gripped the ripples of flesh around her neck and her glasses, (always on a chain) sat nursing the top of her bosom. Flat brogue laced up shoes, also in a variety of colours, were as sturdy and stable as her. She was a kind person with a very matter-of-fact attitude speaking clearly and concisely.

Belinda had known Pamela all her life. When Mini had lived in the town, they had been friends. Pamela was a Gifted One and like Belinda, both sat on the 'Belief Council', the council of leading Gifted Ones. In a way she was a family friend and Belinda felt full of gratitude for having her being in their lives and educating the girls.

"We need to take it to council, Belinda," she asserted, fully aware of Hannah's return as a 'favoured Gifted One.' Naturally she wanted to protect her, along with all the other students.

"I will be sending out mail tonight. School will be closed until further notice. I think I shall refer to it as a 'Viral' outbreak. Do not send the twins in, Belinda! I will ensure that work will be sent out to everybody. Much to do now dear. Oh, give my love to your mother – How is Mini? We need to protect our little Gifted Ones!"

Without Belinda really having chance to reply, Pamela had hung up, back attending to school duties.

Hannah's school did not differentiate between Watchers, Gifted Ones and Naturals. Everyone attended the same school, and their individual diversities were accepted, being treated equally. Different to Mini's neighbourhood, where things it seemed were more segregated. Hannah would soon realise though, that there were hidden depths of division. The strong Watcher foothold in her hometown was more sophisticated than it appeared.

'For where there is good there is always evil.'

This unknown breed of Watcher, winged creatures with the body of a lizard and face and beak of a crow were so different in shape to their counterparts, The Watchercrows in America. What remained the same was their hunger to gain control and seize The Gifted Ones power. *'Since the beginning, they had been watching and waiting.'*

The fact that Ashby-by-the-Sea was a popular tourist hotspot had meant that for decades people passed through the pretty little market town. Of all the postcards written, a tower as tall as the castle could have been built. Only now were some of The Gifted beginning to wonder if all visitors were authentic or prying.

Amelia and many more had clearly become infected during, or maybe even before the summer. These new creepers of the dark realm were quite clearly incredibly invasive, being able to change size. For Naturals life went on as normal, oblivious to the wretchedness that existed above in the air and below the very ground they walked upon. Tim was one of them and for now, he was in his 'attic room' at the top of the house. Not actually in the roof space but nevertheless referred to as 'his' room, as far away as he felt he needed to escape.

It was an eclectic room that served his scientific calling. Belinda steered well clear of it. The untidiness of it alone would send her into a tailspin. She did rather well in overlooking and accepting both Tim and Hannah's ways in this department, which were quite different to hers. Hannah however, rather liked his room. To her it was another world and all a bit, 'mad professor.'

Walking into Tim's room, straight ahead stood a huge wooden work bench in front of a built-in chimney, where long ago the fire-place would have been. Rectangular with long legs, it enabled Tim, a tall slender man to sit for hours, in the comfort of a high-backed leather chair.

Over the years, the bench, which had been inherited from his uncle, had more marks than an oak tree. Not one part of it was ever on view; it was always smothered in papers, pens, and books.

A huge domed chrome light hung over it like some sort of medical lamp hovering over an operating table, revealing paper clips, plans, rulers, and the like. This was where plans were laid out, pondered upon, and scribbled on.

Tim's chair was on wheels, and he would slide across the wooden floor in frantic movements, to the other two large tables which were under the window and on the back wall. Cables from the ceiling hung over each of them with tools galore and more pieces of metal than a car mart or garage. The operations occurred here, and this was where his creations were built.

Joy had spent many a happy hour being operated on, but most of the time her place was by the door on a high-backed wooden chair, where she would recharge.

Next to Joy was the technical backup to Tim's world. A gigantic computer, with three screens stood on an aluminium table. Six strong shelves containing books, magazines and files hung above. The top shelf was the 'I love me shelf' proudly boasting his many achievements from university such as photos, framed certificates, and honorary prizes along with an old Bunsen burner and the odd scientific souvenir. The room had a distinctive metal smell combined with fresh tar and lead. When Tim was building, kitted up in goggles and a stained overcoat, Belinda would yell, "Tim, close the door." as the smell from his work was far reaching.

Tim had never really left his university days as far as his dress was concerned and he lived in jeans, open neck shirt and jersey (nearly always a v-neck jersey). His floppy hair complimented his stereotypical university lecturer look. He often retreated to 'his' room following Belinda's mindful experiences or to the garden to fiddle with his garden pots.

'If you are happy, I am happy.' Tim was one for repeating mantras, this being the one of the moment. It was perhaps a way of him coping with Belinda's and now, his daughters Gifts. Quite clearly a challenge; he could not comprehend nor fathom the 'math' behind being a Gifted One. This intrigue would lead him one day to further investigate.

So, the old market town of Ashby-by-the-Sea was richly blessed with not only Tim, a top scientist, but also with its heritage, landscape, and surrounding areas. Market Street, the one Hannah daydreamed of walking with Tom, was the town's cobbled main street. The many traditional shops that lined it and which she would want to visit with him, were housed in pretty buildings of various period architecture.

Residents made every effort to 'shop local' and participate in town life. It was this lifestyle that bred familiarity and a togetherness she was keen to share with Tom; a stark contrast to the austere neighbourhood he had grown up in. Among the many events organised was a lighting ceremony which took place every Christmas, run by the 'Sea Stars' a voluntary group which worked tirelessly overseeing such town events.

Living in the heart of it all, were the Timms, at No. 12, Upper Bridge Street. They occupied one of the few residential homes in the centre of town, at what locals referred to as the 'high-end.' Or, quite simply put, the top end of Market Street, as it ran uphill. Upper Bridge Street ran parallel to the street at the bottom of Market Street, called Church Street.

Market Street divided the residential areas. Pocklington being on the left side of the Timms' and the homes of The Gifted and Naturals dotted out of the town centre, on the other.

There was also a cluster of homes around an area known as 'The Spinney' and the Naturals homes were interspersed amongst them. In the world of The Watchers and The Gifted Ones, home styles differed around the world. At Mini's, the homes were quite different to Hannah's hometown. In Ashby-by-the-Sea, Gifted homes were all about their sustainability, living in a new or historic home, being in an old market town, every effort was made in maintaining the homes. Her dad often said that living amongst water was challenging in a damp old town. His words ran deeper than he thought. Typical Gifted homes were made of timber; energy efficient, with plenty of large glass windows to let the light in. They were bold, bright, and open, compared with the dark, damp closed homes of The Watchers in Pocklington. Doors to the Gifted homes were always open, this, as they were about to find out, was to their detriment.

Various alleyways ran between the shops, neatly dividing the towns walkways. Towards the very bottom of Market Street, on the left was Harrisons the butchers, ran by Mr. and Mrs. Harrison. It was probably the most uninteresting building to look at in terms of architecture, but for what the building lacked architecturally, the fine facia board and window displays certainly made up for. Their names stretched the length of the shop in black bold inscription against the cream of the board. Mr. Harrison was immensely proud of the vast selection of quality meats he procured, laying them out in full view for passers-by to inspect through the spotlessly clean, large windowpanes. His double fronted glass doors had large, long brass handles in the shape of the letter H. They were heavy and the fitted weather strips made a sucking sound as they snapped tightly shut, keeping the air outside, along with any unwanted insects. They also helped maintain the coolness of the shop, preserving the strong smell of fresh meat.

Mr. Harrison was a tall man with a thick moustache. His thick woolly snood, that he always wore, met the ends of his moustache and his apron fitted tightly over what seemed to be at least a couple of layers of sweaters, due to the coolness of his shop.

Mrs. Harrison, by comparison, was tiny and looked minute behind the counter. She wore a cardigan over her apron that seemed to dangle down towards her ankles. She served the sliced meats, cheese, pates, and of course her renowned steak pies, which always had a 'H', made from pastry, on the top. Her gentle tone was befitting to her delicate frame and counteracted Mr. Harrison's deep voice as he hacked the limbs of his prized mutton.

Belinda and Tim were regulars at Harrisons butchers, taking it in turn to pick up whatever was Belinda's dish of the day. Often it was Tim, as across the cobbles was the Post Office, run with extreme efficiency by none other than the Cox's. Tim was a regular there and friends with Mr. Cox. A bald man of average height and casually dressed, Mr. Cox's stationary knowledge would surpass all, and the stock in his shop was exemplary. He was particularly knowledgeable on the logistics of international freight and chatty to all who visited the shop, knowing almost all the locals by their first names.

His wife, Mrs. Cox, was the Vicar of 'Star of the Sea' on Church Street. Time was of the essence for her as she was preoccupied with yielding goodness and light into the lives of others. One could not miss her, because whatever the season, she would always wear extremely bright, colourful clothes, in all the colours of the rainbow. Locals would say, there goes Mrs. Cox, as one could not miss her passing by.

It was her sense of speed that was most compelling, she spoke and walked with immense velocity and quite clearly, always on a mission. Her entire body, or so it seemed, was built to accommodate this fast spiritedness that she harnessed. She was tall with pointy features and her long nose thrusted her forward into action.

And finally, as it is important to share with you these notable shops on Market Street, there was the fishmongers, the bakers, and the chemist. The fishmongers was near the butchers and the Post Office, whilst the bakers and chemist were towards the top end of the Street.

Mrs. Robinson, the fishmonger was widowed, her face was as sad as the poor trout which lay on the cold slabs of her shop. Her black attire, worn through a life of mourning, only added to her gloomy persona.

The facer board of the shop once signified a couple wholeheartedly in business, but since Mr. Robinson's untimely death and following years of neglect, the 'in' in 'Robinson' had fallen away, it now read *'Mr. & Mrs Rob son.'* The shop lacked maintenance and cracks had appeared in the facade. The locals tried to overlook her gloominess and supported the shop regardless.

And then there was the Bakers, ran by Ben and Dale. Perhaps one of the prettiest shops on the street with a yellow and cream awning that extended over the pavement.

The delicious smell of freshly baked bread oozed onto the street along with the sweet smell from the pastries and cakes, all of which complimented the nearby cafés coffee aroma just a stone throws away.

A happy pair, Ben and Dale, each with their initials 'D&B' monogrammed on their polo shirts, were reliable, hardworking, and content, if not a little reserved at times. They appeared nonchalant, but this did not distract from the comfort that a bakery often seems to provide for people.

Then lastly was Don Surlin, the Chemist. His shop frontage was bland, apart from a large store sign displaying the image of a snake and a bowl. Flanking the shop, it was visible from both sides.

Don sat behind the black high counter at the back of the shop and did not really say much, only muttering when spoken to. A surly character with jet black hair and deep-set eyes that rarely made any contact with his customers.

Being of a small stature, his white overcoat seemed to drown him. Most locals had concluded that he must be both incredibly diligent as well as intelligent in his selected field, which was why he perhaps didn't converse much. Hannah and Amelia would always say how they got goosebumps in his shop.

Market Street for many was seen through rose tinted spectacles. But all was not as it appeared. Hannah would soon decipher and find out just who was who, to help her she would be attending a very different kind of school in the approaching Michaelmas term, 'The School of Belief.'

Chapter Four

Panther Fairies

As tension built amongst The Gifted, the spirit of Parky had been moved by the Great Star. A few weeks had now passed since Hannah returned home.

Lying on her bed, staring at the blank ceiling, the light from the lampshade cast a long, pointy shadow that reached towards the bedroom door.

Outside, a flurry of leaves swirled, twirled, and whirled in a mad frenzy, with no escape. In their loyal groups, they bounced off the garden walls like deranged balls in a pinball machine.

Hannah was feeling similar, she wondered if Amelia may be feeling the same. It was astounding, she thought, at how much 'lighter' her sister had become over the last few weeks, losing the hard façade and enjoying many a happy hour with her newfound Gift. Having herself witnessed Amelia with Joy, her new imaginary friend, the Amazonian princess; Hannah smiled, it was great that they both now believed, and Amelia had finally become Gifted. Belinda and Mini, both strong women, had nurtured the girls so well, only to have their plans severely disrupted when this intrusive type of Watcher had intervened.

'How annoying' thought Hannah.

Since discovering her own Gift, Hannah had become self-aware and increasingly more perceptive. It had led her to noticing Amelia and Joy's focus on her pendent as well as a feeling that Amelia may be harbouring jealousy toward her.

It was a hinderance in the development of The Gifted, that their own outstanding Gifts sometimes appeared less glamorous to other's Gifts. As such, comparisons were made, and resentments could start to creep in.

The Great Star sadly witnesses Gifted Ones at this vulnerable stage time and time again, and The Watchers prancing upon them. It had already occurred in Hannah's family, with Doodle, Mini's twin, and Victor who had once been a close friend to them both.

For now, at the Timms, as the leaves danced outside, both young women were adjusting to a new way of life. When Belinda had explained school would be closed until further notice, she had glanced over to Tim giving him the look of '*Its Gifted business*' he knew to step back. He would be filled in later.

"Look darlings," she had begun to say, with an arm dangling over each of them. They had been sitting on the stairs, underneath their grandparent's portrait, with Belinda on the step above. Hannah had glanced up at Mini's portraiture and seen her wink back. This sprinkling of magic had been going on from time to time since she'd arrived home. She knew that guided by The Great Star, Mini was able to communicate with her, just as her mother had when she was away.

"We need to sit tight and limit our time outside girls. Protect one another and trust the Star. Mrs. Gives and the council will keep me updated with everything I need to know. We don't fully understand yet, how these types of Watchers work or, how The Gifted Ones are being infected and sleep walking to the castle. In time, all will be revealed."

She then went onto kiss the top of Amelia's head. Belinda and Hannah both knew she was by far the most vulnerable in the family. It was this air of helplessness that seemed to inexplicably excuse her faults.

Having got to know Mini over the summer, Hannah suddenly realised just how similar her mother was to her in many ways. Something like school being cancelled would have once been an issue that would have unsettled her, naturally liking everything to be orderly.

Belinda had learned over the years that being controlling was a negative trait. This was something that Amelia would also struggle with.

In Hannah's room, the shadows on the ceiling were getting longer as the sun outside was setting. She could feel herself drifting off to sleep.

The pendent began to glow, its copper colour appeared the colour of bright amber and slowly began to pulsate. Almost, but not quite sleeping, she entered an unusual, imaginary situation. Her energy levels rose, and the familiar huge tunnel of light appeared to beam out from the middle of her chest. Her imagination was coming to life. All her subconscious thoughts had accumulated into a semi-conscious dream.

This is what occurred. The long shadows from the lampshade had formed into a gigantic star. All dimensions of her bedroom, as before in the kitchen, were lost. Posters swallowed into a vast open space which surrounded her. The star's long narrow rays spiked forward thrusting into the unknown. Hannah felt her body being lifted from the bed, propelled by the pendant. The panther seemed to detach from the necklace, growing life-size and hovering ahead in the wide-open space. Appearing for the first time since she had returned home, she found herself standing upright, facing Parky now a full-sized panther.

"Parky!" she said happily, extending her arms to embrace him, but the space around him was ethereal, so she couldn't.

As he turned around, his tail swished, and the copper colour refracted in the light of the Star. Turning his back to Hannah he raised his front paw, beckoning her to follow him and the Star, which was moving through the space. As she followed the space shifted and formed a dome like dimension. Below the dome were multiple bending waterways, and rising from them, breaking though the top of the almighty dome, rose a castle. It was Ashby castle, and it was beginning to consume the entire space at speed. Feeling restricted, her heart began to race, her energy faded and everything around her dispersed into dust. Taking a swift sharp breath in, beads of sweat dripped from her forehead down her nose. The sweat and salty taste made her squint closing her eyes. Upon opening them she was once again staring at her bedroom ceiling.

At No.12, Upper Bridge Street that evening, it wasn't only Hannah who was adapting to the new chapter in her life; everybody was. With all the twists and turns that were to unfold as the unfathomable experiences abounded for The Gifted, in preparation for the battle ahead, Tim was dutifully doing his bit as well. Baffled by Belinda's description of the new Watchers, Tim thought how he may be able to help his girls fight off this new unfathomable fiend. At this stage for him, the new invasion was all in the mind, everything outside of science was never challenged. He set to work on Joy's sensors so that she could begin to detect large insect type creatures, as Belinda had described them to him.

As the light from his large lamp shone from his attic room, as he kindly set the sensors, Hannah was still lying on her bed, struggling to dispel the thoughts from her mind, of the exact unwanted guests he was working on, she was piecing it all together, keeping it to herself, sharing it she thought, may further rumble the already unsettled come confused feeling in the house. Maturely, she decided patiently to wait in the hope it would lead to a clearer picture, and as it turned out it was a wise choice.

The next morning, just as the cuckoo clock chimed nine, the post clunked through the letterbox, thudding to the floor. Delivered in the safe hands by Bob the postman, who everybody in town knew, probably because he spent as much time chatting as delivering.

The smell of coffee, the rustling of papers and the clashing of breakfast crockery, along with the undertone of Joy's movements echoed from the kitchen through the hallway and a sense of normality, momentarily returned.

"I'll collect it!" Amelia said, running down the stairs.

The post was nearly always for Tim, but as in most households the surprise of mail being delivered, commands a magical suspense that only Christmas morning can equal. It is the privilege of the collector to thumb through the mail, which often Amelia greedily feasted upon.

"Dad. Dad. Mum. Dad. Dad. Science junk," she churned through the pile like speed counting bank notes. The climax of coming to the end of the pile was fast approaching, "Han!" Amelia cried back up the stairs, "there's one for us!"

Joy made her way into the hall, programmed by Tim to respond to the sound of the letter box dropping mail. Amelia half-heartedly handed her the unimportant post before remembering her manners. "Oh, thanks Joy." Becoming her imaginary friend, she held a new affection for her which went beyond her AI duties to the family.

Amelia parked herself on the stairs placing Hannah's letter beside her.

"What we got?" Hannah said as she skipped and jumped down the stairs before picking up the letter and plonking herself alongside Amelia. As she shuffled up closely to her, Amelia sat upright fidgeting slightly away. Hannah's natural exuberance and scruffy appearance as they had grown older annoyed her.

"Looks like they are from Mini." Amelia said suggestively, flipping her letter back and forth.

International mail. Mr. Cox would be in heaven! thought Hannah.

For a moment both girls paused and looked at each other. Curiously to the right and slightly above, a hazy glow wrapped a shaft of light, casting itself down in front of them. It was coming diagonally from the portrait of their grandparents.

In that instant both of their imaginations started to come to life. Crystallised in the twin's minds, their grandmother, oceans away, had intuitively been ready for this important moment. As their energy rose, the light from their chests beamed.

Hannah looked at Amelia. It was only the second time she had witnessed her in this way and memories came flooding back of her own imagination coming to life. She was still in awe thinking about it and her pendant glowed.

"Hello Hannah and now Amelia! I am so happy about that." Mini said joyfully, covered in a cloudy haze.

Amelia was all smiles peering up at Mini. In the past, pangs of jealously had prevented her from this now natural exuberance and the air of judgment about her grandmother being 'barmy' had dropped.

Many Gifted Ones can be portrayed in this manner. When the light of a Gifted One smashes into the dark, it can be overwhelming for some. To bright, too light. Many are taken aback with the light, unable to accept and overwhelmed with the contrast. A Gifted One now herself, she gazed up in admiration as though Mini was a Queen holding court. Reminding them both of their Gifted obligations, Mini said,

'Because to see girls, you have to truly believe...'

Meanwhile, Belinda in the kitchen with Tim, was fully aware of the 'goings on' in the hallway. She had found it liberating when the girls had both finally become Gifted. This was thanks in part to her mother, who having been widowed, she was extremely close to, especially growing up without a father. They had shared a lifetime supporting one another. It had resulted in Belinda becoming responsible and highly organised if not, as we know, somewhat controlling. Mini cherished their Gifted bond, particularly not having the privilege of being nurtured by her own parents. She had often wondered if perhaps being Gifted was not discussed in her day. Mini had been nurtured by a higher source in discovering her Gifted power.

"Go on girls, open them!" Mini exclaimed, full of energy and light in her usual compelling manner. What was about to occur was more than a sprinkling of magic.

As each simultaneously opened their letters, instantly recognisable as Mini's personalised stationary with two engraved palm trees intertwined at the top, tiny, winged panthers flew from out of each envelope. Hannah's pendant began to pulsate. One, two, three, tiny panthers, from each envelope, fluttered out flying around the hallway. Soon there were up to twenty. Both girls looked on in glee. Amelia put her hands out trying to touch them; they were like panther fairies. Soon both girls dropped their letters and were all fingers and thumbs fumbling their way through the air, trying in vain to catch the feline fairies as their tiny wings flapped ferociously. It was as though they had both returned to their childhood, chasing butterflies.

"He's always with us girls!" Mini said, chuckling, overlooking their delight, before calming the frenzy.

"Now, now, Hannah, please sit, darling and read aloud your letter. They are both the same."

It read like this,

My Dearest Hannah and Amelia,

You may think it odd that the writer of the letter spectates the reader, but by being present I hope it emphasizes the importance of its contents.

I have important news. The Watchers, threatened by the Spirit of Parky, are preparing a revengeful comeback and The Gifted Ones are in danger.

Hannah, you must use your skills and power which you have recently acquired to investigate immediately.

Together with your imaginary friends, both of you, use each other's strengths to raise one another up. Doodle and I never had such an opportunity to work together towards a world without Watchers. You have this chance. Be careful though, do not let earths needs and desires control your mission.

Now, since you are both automatically in the School of Belief, it is incredibly important Hannah, as a favoured one, you join the Belief Council with your mother. The Leader is a friend of mine called Ann, she is blind but can see the state of souls. She will help you in your quest.

Lastly, remember, 'Be careful of what you allow into your mind.'

Always together in heart. Mini, Wink. X

Finishing the letter, Hannah looked up towards Mini, but the cloudy haze was dispersing as were the tiny panthers. Before long she was back in the portrait, frozen in time, just as Belinda the portrait used to be, and the panthers gone. 'So, that explains the weird dream in my bedroom.' She thought.

Both girls sat dazed with their letters flopped down over their knees. They were bewildered by the contrast of such sheer delight to disturbing news. Then, Amelia narrowing her eyes, snapped out of her stunned state, and looking directly at Hannah's pendent, in a demanding desperate tone said, "tell me more about Parky. Now!"

As so many times in the past, the Watchers were watching and waiting to crush the Gifted and unbeknown, they were everywhere.

Chapter Five

The Belief Council

Hannah's steely character tried hard to ignore Amelia's demanding direct manner, in which she asked about her beloved panther. Even though at the time it had reminded her of seeing Victor imprinted upon her face.

"Parky is a gift from the Great Star, unlike any other; a gift for everyone in the world!"

Hannah chose joy in obliging to Amelia's request and happily regaled all she knew about the special panther.

"Miraculous beyond belief is how Mini describes him. He really is Amelia, he really is. He, he's alive!" Her pendant began to glow.

"You know the huge shelf I told you he's on at Mini's? Well, in the summer, our Gifted power made him alive. Even though The Watchers destroyed him, he came back to life!"

"W o w." Amelia replied slowly and sarcastically, staring at the pendant.

"I've even flown on his back! He's super special!"

She noticed Amelia's eyes spitefully narrowing again as she continued to stare, it was making her feel uncomfortable. Deciding to kindly confront her she said,

"Yes. Mini gave the necklace to me. I really believe the pendant is him, well his spirit anyway."

Amelia flicked her hair several times as Hannah sat in silence trying to work out if she was jealous about the fact Mini had given her the necklace or if her attitude was related to The Watchers or now being Gifted. Amelia appeared confident, but she wasn't. Like Tim, flicking her hair was a habit, one she usually did when she felt insecure or if she was being arrogant, which was probably in defence of an unsure situation.

Hannah, perturbed by Amelia, still enjoyed their chat. It was rare they talked openly about anything these days. She hadn't even told her properly about Tom yet. It would be something she would share with her gently, for as far as she was aware, Amelia hadn't had a boyfriend yet. She had thought from time-to-time what Tom would think of her and vice versa. Now back home, she came to realise they had a lot in common. Hannah was beginning to understand stronger Gifted Ones like herself, attracted the needy. *It was the way of The Star to shine and serve.*

Before long, Belinda from the kitchen was calling, "Come on girls." Breakfast was ready and she knew Mini had worked her magic.

What a way to start the day in the Timms household. Much

more lay ahead and much more was about to be revealed. Practically, Belinda amongst other things had an online art class, which Hannah, after completing her schoolwork, would participate in along with Joy. A joint love of art was their thing, but before then Belinda had other things on her mind. She wanted to know from the girls about Mini's letter, already knowing its contents. Her letter was the bridge to what she was about to empower them with on the next stage of their Gifted journey, knowledge about The Belief Council.

She dashed around the kitchen at considerable speed, very much like Mini, grabbing the appropriate utensils like some skilled ninja, whilst looking up at Cork from time to time, saying, "It's time to believe." A phrase that the girls, Hannah in particular, would come to learn was used at The Belief Council.

After breakfast, like so many times before, they sat around the kitchen table. Tim had nestled nicely into reading, having moved onto 'AI monthly.' Even though Amelia was not sitting on the Belief Council, she was nevertheless included in Belinda's debrief learning all about it.

With her back straight, Belinda sat with such incredible poise. Crossing her hands, she raised and lowered them onto the table. She was about to chair one of the most important meetings of her life, with the most important people *in* her life.

But just as Belinda dropped her hands to the table, Amelia spontaneously got up and went to hug her. It was strange as you would think her standoffish attitude would not allow such a display of affection, but this was common practice for Amelia. Hannah wondered, being self-assured in her given affections, if Amelia did this to make up for her usual brusque manner, to remind her loved ones she cared. It seemed she was always thinking about Amelia lately, trying endlessly to work her out. She didn't need to. She needed to just concentrate on the task in hand.

In her husky tones and in a formal manner Belinda began,

"Belief Councils exist worldwide. Just as The Watchers sought their own network of 'Spectacle' council's centuries ago, so did The Gifted Ones. The Belief and The Spectacle both have particularly strong footholds here, because of the history of the castle. It being the final resting place of The Great Gifted Nickolous, the father of all Watchers, as well as the breeding ground for this deadly type of Watcher.

"The current leader of the Belief Council is Ann, the elderly lady who lives with her dog in Jigsaw Cottage down the road."

Hannah and Amelia passed this house almost every day of their lives. A little further up from theirs, from the outside it was a ramshackle of a place, dilapidated in appearance, but being placed on the corner of Upper Bridge Street, it held the finest views of Market Street.

"Oh, I know the one." Hannah said.

"Oh yeah," Amelia added, "The one always with the flowers in the window."

"Yes, quite right darling, Ann treats her sense of smell with a fresh delivery of flowers every week, according to the season. Mini knew Ann during her time here and together they served on the council. She's eighty-four years old now."

"Does she have a dog?" Hannah thought she may have seen one patiently waiting outside the shops, and Ann fumbling to untie him.

"Yes, but it's not a guide dog, I think it is a mongrel. You did know Ann is blind?" Both girls knew and nodded, "Oh, I nearly forgot. Joy can you record this please?" "Yes, Belinda, I can record this conversation." She replied melodically. "Thank you, dear."

"Good, I'm pleased you're using that option." Tim muttered, face down flicking the pages of his magazine.

"So, carrying on, yes, Ann is blind, but her power being a Gifted One, she can see the state of peoples souls."

Tim had a disinterested look but held a perky ear, raising his eyebrows when details got 'juicy.' Now was one of those moments, even though he would have probably known the information. Amelia certainly got her cynical approach from him.

"What does that mean?" Hannah asked inquisitively.

"Well, The Great Star has enabled Ann to see the state of a person's soul; their consciousness. Hence the name of her home, Jigsaw Cottage. Piecing it all together, I guess you could say, doing jigsaws of the mind."

Ann was a short lady who needed a frame to aid her mobility. Walter her dog always walked loyally at her pace. Always plainly dressed, she had a soft mysterious face, with gentle features. Her head hosted a brain unlike any other.

"So, is she in charge of the council then?" Amelia asked, ever inquisitive.

"Yes, leaders are guided by The Great Star to answer their calling and to carefully appoint and select eleven others. Each of whom wear, 'The necklace of Belief.'

Belinda pulled hers out from under her sweater to show the girls.

"You'll be getting yours soon Hannah," smiling at her warmly.

"Yeah, to add to the collection." Amelia spitefully remarked.

Belinda blinked her eyes slowly. She tolerated the way they bickered.

Hannah did her best to also ignore the remark, as it made her slightly angry and defensive.

She recalled similar feelings in the summer with Tom. It was around the time The Watchers were manipulating him. Again, a similar feeling she had with Tom, when manipulated by The Watchers he looked to use Parky. These similarities with Tom and Amelia were becoming more obvious. Both these people were close and dear to her, whilst confused. It only increased the burning desire deep inside her to meet this mission. As in the summer though, necessary groundwork had to be done. It was again the way of The Star. *Timing: There is a time for everything.*

The delicately made gold chain necklace had the word 'Believe' hanging at the bottom of the chain.

"There is also a process of introspection. Which..."

"What's introspection?" Amelia interrupted mid-sentence.

"The meaning of introspection. Introspection is the examination or observation of one's own mentality and emotion. Shall I continue?" Joy was programmed to intercede openly asked questions, a useful option often used by the girls for school.

"No, thank you Joy. There you go girls, expertly delivered by Joy as usual. It is a kind of mental, self-care check. Ann is particularly good at tending to the flock and never lauds it over." Belinda explained.

"Now, where were we," going onto explain, "oh yes, the council convenes at Jigsaw Cottage.

"Looks tiny!" Amelia interrupted. "How do they all fit in there?!" smirking at Tim, who grinned back.

"Well, it is a mystery of faith and only for true believers. So, are you both ready to find out?"

Both girls nodded eagerly.

"At the back of Ann's house, through her bright airy rooms is a conservatory. Simple interiors aid her mobility, so it is easy to access. You are right, the space is tight, but once one or more Gifted Ones are gathered in the conservatory, the area begins to expand into a vast open space where all dimensions of the existing room are lost. An endless space, with no limitations, in idyllic settings that hold a tranquillity beyond measure. Gentle flowing waterfalls, lush green gardens, rolling hills and valleys. Meadows full of wildflowers and fruits aplenty. Multiple shafts of light break through branches within thick abundant forests. Lakes stretch serenely into oceans towards a never-ending horizon. Oh, I could go on, it is quite simply the crown of glory that never fades away."

Everyone was grossly engaged in Belinda's description and Hannah's pendant was glowing. Even Tim had put his magazine down although he had heard it all before. Somehow it held even more significance now that both of his daughters were a part of it. Perhaps the least interested was Amelia because she was distracted by Hannah's necklace. Despite this, both said how amazing it all sounded, which pleased Belinda who believed that appreciation of creation tended to come with maturity.

Hannah felt there was a similarity to the description of the open space to her dream and to the time in the kitchen when all their imaginations had ignited together. Her thoughts were soon distracted when Belinda said,

"Time really is of the essence; The Watchers activity is brewing, and the council will soon assemble again. Mrs. Gives is acting secretary and she will inform me." It suddenly dawned upon both girls that Mrs Gives, their headmistress, was on the Belief Council.

When Mini left Ashby-by-the-Sea for America, she had entrusted Belinda's care to her good friends at the council, believing them all to be spiritual brothers and sisters. First though, she had nurtured Belinda's Gift and shared with her the myth of the Watcherguards laying their eggs in the crypt of The Great Gifted Nickolous as well as the new type of Watcher, The Flying Watcherfish. With her profound trust in The Great Star, she felt her daughter was at no risk and soon afterwards returned to America.

"Who else is on that council?" Tim asked slightly cocky.

"Oh, Tim, I'm sure I have told you before. Let me think, well, there will be Hannah and I. Mrs. Gives and Ann, that is four. Then, let me see, there are Mr. and Mrs. Harrison from the Butchers and Mr. Cox from the post office. Oh yes, and Mrs. Cox from the Church. So that is eight and those lovely couples..., now, what are their names, oh yes, Mary and Maria and Mike and Madge. I think that makes twelve.

The others had lost interest as Belinda rattled on, but Tim, albeit slightly sarcastically, dropped what he was reading and went onto to say,

"Well, the sooner your council meets the better. Old Cox was acting out of character the other day when I went in to return some wires to be shipped internationally."

"In what way, he's always so perky and chatty?" Belinda asked quizzically.

"Ha! He is certainly not that way now. He seemed preoccupied, grumpy and look worried."

"Well, he would have been briefed about The Watchers, although I do know what you mean, nothing tends to ruffle his feathers usually".

Listening to her parent's conversation, Hannah was unaware that soon she would be having an important conversation with her father that would assist them both in what was going to be a challenge unlike any other. Letting things unfurl like this and following her intuition, even at times in the next few days the impulse to start investigating was unbearable, created a newfound acceptance in Hannah of the unknown, allowing another week to pass, opening October's door.

Undeterred by the bitter battle brewing between The Watchers and The Gifted Ones, many, in particularly the Naturals of the town, had ironically started to display Halloween décor. The dark nights bought the undeniable smell of autumn, the musky smell of burnt wood and the crisp air complemented the cobwebbed and hunched 'stringy' black cats hanging in the windows, just some of the decorations on show. There was still a distinct smell of algae, although the change of season had somehow oppressed it pungency.

The 'Sea Stars' effort for the town didn't disappoint and Market Street always seemed to have a 'Dickensian feel' about it during the holiday season. From Halloween through to Christmas, it was something that brought delight to people of all ages living in the town. The squeals and gasps of children could be heard echoing through the town for most of the month.

Shop owners made a tremendous effort, even dressing the part. The Harrisons often scattered scary spiders amongst the meat and Mrs. Harrison forwent the 'H' on her pies, letting a long-legged arthropod take the highlight instead. Mr. Harrison even wore a scary mask for Halloween.

"Careful those pies aren't full of the crawly things!" he'd say in jest. Mrs. Harrison would silently chuckle. Even Ben and Dale made 'skull' cupcakes and a warming blood-like soup was always bubbling away, perfect for the chillier evenings.

Finally, a date had been set for the Belief Council to satisfy Hannah's itch to begin her exploration and find out more about The Watchers formidable plans. She wondered how her mother was feeling about having her girls on the council. Unlike her concerns for Amelia, she knew her mother would simply be putting her trust in The Great Star. As it would happen, letting things unfurl in their own time, they both received a letter from the council instructing them to isolate.

On a type of papyrus, with the word 'Believe' imprinted in gold, at the top, it read:

Believe

Dear friends,

To help combat The Watchers, remain at home with your imaginary friends and build up mindful strength. I am fully aware this type of Watcher comes in an unusual shape and size to that of the crow, and indeed have already breached some homes. My advice is to remain vigilant and only use your power, for now, at home. This should hopefully reduce their ability to detect our mindful energy and thus, their ability to cruelly destroy aspects of it.

'Sleep walking believers' are being affected daily by The Watchers, being led to the castle. Why, we do not yet know, but what we do know is that we must continue to trust that all will be revealed, hopefully at our next gathering. Keep shining bright!

Yours

Ann

P.S Thanks to Mrs. Gives for her support with this letter and being able to continue to guide you all.

Important as the letter was, it would be a meeting with 'magic Mini' that would set Hannah on her path, reminding her of her Gifted obligations, but just before that, it was time for 'that' conversation with her father.

Following the arrival of the letter from the Belief Council, Joy was back on the 'operating table' as Tim, goggles on, investigated her sensors. Hannah was with him in the attic room chatting, also wearing a pair of goggles, as the red light above the door signified Dad was at work and it was compulsory when the light was on to grab a pair from the plastic box outside his room.

It was towards the end of the day and being dark outside, many lit lamps gave the room a surgical feel like an operating theatre. Fixing Joy was a job in addition to Tim's 'current' project of the day. As we know, Hannah would often participate in deep chats with her father, and whilst watching him attend to Joy, thoughts came to her. It was so kind of him to fix Joy's sensors, to detect things which he himself didn't believe existed.

"Have you ever been 'Gifted' Dad? Or wanted to believe?"

Putting down his tools, he ran his hands through his hair and taking off his goggles looked at Hannah quite seriously and said,

"It's not for me Han. Not that I would ever stop you, Amelia, or your mother, but I lean more towards science than unfathomable power."

Asking the question, her pendant took on a glow and began to pulsate. Hannah felt he didn't really mean what he was saying and feeling strangely warm, her energy began to rise, and her imagination came to life.

Tim seeing her distracted goggled up and continued his work.

Parky the panther sprung full size from the pendant onto the cluttered floor of Tim's room, as a light poured from out of her chest.

"Oh Dad, I really wish you did believe." she said walking off, flinging her goggles into the pot, following her beloved panther down the stairs.

It was quite simply magnificent seeing a full-sized panther walking freely in her home. As she passed Amelia's room, she saw her at her desk, head down, still deep in schoolwork; for a moment she felt naughty. Amelia's imaginary friend was being fixed.

As she approached the bottom of the stairs, Parky halted. Perching sideways on one of the steps he sat looking up at Mini's portrait. Then, in a flash, he'd jumped straight into the frame to where Mini could be seen standing on her own, in what looked like a big top circus tent. She petted her beloved Panther, who in return licked and nuzzled her.

"Hey boy, I only saw you a moment ago!" Her voice was shriller, and her grandfather was nowhere to be seen. This was because during this time of her life, her circus days, she was sixteen and had not yet met him. Hannah had become a bystander, gazing into the portrait. Mini stood casually dressed in flare fitting jeans, a tight t-shirt, with a polka dot scarf tied around her neck. Pentheus the leopard came sashaying by.

'Aww Pentheus', thought Hannah. It was wonderful to see him again. He had been crushed and stolen from The Gifted Ones imagination in the Battle of Minds that summer.

Mini was now sitting on a bale of straw as a few clowns walked by. Up ahead a trapeze artist seemed to be warming up and behind Mini a young woman could be seen walking towards her. Seeing Mini was with the big cats, the woman's eyes narrowed. Hannah began to recognise who it was. The young Doodle, Mini's twin. The big cats both continued to caress Mini, showering her with love and Doodle walked away. Parky then spoke to Mini, looking directly at her and in the same distinctive deep and meaningful voice said,

"The Great Star has provided the 'favoured' Gifted Ones with exemplary imaginative friends. No Gifted One is without companion or friend, but *only if you believe with your full heart can your imagination come to life,"* reminding Mini of her Gifted obligations to visit her new friends often.

In those early days Mini had clearly discovered she was a Gifted One as she freely conversed with the animals. Parky had given Hannah the exact same message in the summer as they both sat on the shelf at Mini's. '*To Believe.*'

As a cloudy haze returned the portrait back to her grandparents, Hannah realised it was time.

Queen Nail, her imaginary new friend was waiting for her. So was Cork, the stag in the kitchen, and Joy, the Amazonian Princess.

It was time and the Watchers were waiting.

Chapter Six

A Royal Palm

A heavy frost clung to the garden casting its silver net far and wide, tickling Queen Nail's crown and glazing the pond. From the back of the house, the steam from the pipes bellowed out, its dewy spawn melting the frozen sugar-coated glow.

In the dark depths of the previous night, Amelia had been sleepwalking towards the castle, but was stopped before she had wandered too far. At the time and unbeknown to all, it was part of a perfect plan as The Great Star works in mysterious ways. For the Timms though, it really was the last straw and annoyingly, Joy's systems were incapable of detecting the ghastly new breed of Watcher.

A forlorn feeling hung heavy over the house. Amelia was sitting in her bedroom, casually messing with her stuff. Her love of fashion and fussing over her things meant she spent much time pottering. Lately though, her Gift had distracted her from material pleasures, and she had been enjoying many a happy hour with Joy, in an imaginative blissful state. Belinda had also been exercising her mind producing paintings of Cork. This period was important, as the time would soon come, as before, when The Gifted Ones would have to rely on their imaginary friends.

Hannah ventured into the garden in her slippers, her dressing gown wrapped tightly around her, as it was chilly. As the cold silently whipped around her, she stood looking at Queen Nail, statuesque and laden with frost.

This Queen was about to play an essential role in history in the battle against The Watchers. Needed by all, she was a gift from The Great Star, beyond all human reckoning. Hannah would become unconditionally united with her.

As her energy rose and her imagination came to life, Hannah's pendant began to glow intensely. The light beaming from the middle of this favoured Gifted One's chest seemed stronger and brighter than ever before, shinning so bright in the presence of her extraordinary imaginary friend.

In no time at all, Queen Nail shimmering and shining, had transformed. Her silver hair seemed to waft in a gentle breeze, caused by the flapping of her mermaid tail. Hovering mid-air once again, her crown of stars, set amidst the morning frost, was truly spectacular, giving her the aura of an ice queen.

"Hannah my dear" she said gently, extending her arms forward, revealing her glistening long blue nails. Then as before, she turned her palms to face upwards. "As you embark on this journey of discovery, I will endeavour to navigate you."

Moving to hover over the pond, she beckoned Hannah to join her.

"Look at my palms" she said. The creases had transfigured into tiny waterways, some more pronounced than others. Hannah looked on in astonishment watching the water flow in the lines of her hands. "Things are different to what The Great Star intended."

And then, as if magically listening, in the clear morning sky above, appeared The Great Star of the Cosmos. Its long narrow rays touched the garden walls, and its pulsating core caused its rays to dazzle.

In the presence of such unfathomable activity, Hannah felt the strength of her power radiating deep within her; it made her look down towards her necklace. The pendant was so radiant, she could hardly keep her eyes open from the blinding white light, yet she could still see Queen Nail hovering in her peripheral vision.

"Our connection is vital dear," she exclaimed. "The little streams you see should flow perfectly and be crystal clear, ebbing and flowing as intended. These are the tributaries for larger dramatic sources of water. The huge source of water at the end has immense power, but without the smaller streams it would not exist. Your hometown features many waterways."

As she began to say this, the waterways on her palms began to reflect the brooks and streams of Ashby-by-the-Sea. The brook was of course the 'Gillaweep'. It fed from higher ground by a series of waterfalls. Hannah knew of it, as she and Amelia had played there when they were younger. It flowed right through Pocklington, into parts of the town underground. Far behind the waterfalls, existed the caves that she'd only ever heard about.

"The water you see no longer runs clear, it has become infected, dirty and stagnant. Left stale for The Watchers gain. This corruption of creation has occurred as they have evolved, enabling them to prey on Gifted Ones in a different way." Her gracious face, gently saddened.

"At Mini's, The Watchers haunted the skies." Replied Hannah.

"Yes, Watchercrows exist here too," Queen Nail affirmed, lowering her palms down. "Now, we are tormented above and below."

During this imaginary encounter, as The Great Star shone on, an incredible transmission of immense powers occurred between Hannah and her imaginary friend. Queen Nail was now spiritually interconnected with her thought processes and able to read Hannah's mind.

She instantly responded to her thoughts of 'why, how, when, what' in relation to the Watcher's presence in her hometown,

"Now you are enlightened Hannah; Everything has changed and needs to, in order to enable the muddy waters to run clean." Hannah drew in a deep breath before peering up at The Great Star. Queen Nail continued, "You need to stay strong and be prepared at all times, with your full Gifted armour ready. Remember, only if you truly believe in your Gift can you take your stand against The Watchers cunning schemes. Our struggle is against the powers of their dark world, so that on the day The Great Gifted Nickolous returns, we may stand our ground. Do you still have the Book of Spells?"

"Yes, of course." she replied.

Small enough to fit in the palm of a hand, it was leather bound in red with gilt edging and a golden clasp. Hannah had kept it under her pillow from the day Tom had emotionally returned it to her. This tiny book held immense power and had helped Tom in the battle against The Watchers, but more than this, it also healed his relationship with Hannah, sealing a once broken trust. In the act of forgiveness for his misdemeanour, they had fallen in love. They had experienced so many strong feelings in a relatively short period of time.

"The Book of Spells can be used again, Hannah," Queen Nail confirmed, "but remember; carefully." Then, smiling warmly, she looked up towards The Great Star before plunging seamlessly, in a vertical pencil dive, into the pond.

Hannah's dazzling white pendant returned to its former state as she wrapped her dressing gown tightly around her. The experience had increased the chill in the air, provoking memories of her recent dreams. Now that it had been revealed that Queen Nail would navigate her in the treacherous waters which lay ahead, everything seemed to be building up, somewhat linking together, in preparation for her to jump into action. Mini had warned her when she told her, '*Troubles will carve your inner star to shine even brighter.*'

For some reason, before she headed back into the kitchen, she decided to turn, looking up to her bedroom window. Peering out was the face of Victor, his mean inset eyes pierced right through her. An icy feeling made her shiver, jumping out of her own skin, blinking several times, but in seconds he was gone… Replaced instead by Amelia, staring back blanky. Feeling unhinged and thinking she must be seeing things, smiling bravely she raised her hand to wave at Amelia, then head down, hurried back into the house and the kitchen.

Sitting with Tim, beautifully upright at the table, was Joy. Her inbuilt encyclopaedia was reeling off what sounded like an explanation of a story which Tim was reading from the broad sheet papers, opened out in front of him. Leaning slightly back with his head tilted, he was listening intensely to what she was relaying. In a rather lazy manner, recognising Hannah had come in from the garden, he muttered,

"Err morning Han, chilly out there? Your mum has popped into town with Amelia, to get some milk. I said I would have gone but…" He stopped mid-sentence, bending his ear to Joy catching an important part of the story.

Hannah knew they were back, only moments earlier she had waved to Amelia. Heading upstairs to the chime of the cuckoo clock, she took two steps at a time to warm up.

"What were you doing in my room Amelia?!" Hannah said in jest, without looking, as she passed by Amelia's room. It was a petty remark, but it was annoying she thought, that she had gone into her room without asking. Had it been the other way around Amelia would have been in a right strop. Without waiting for a response, she carried on to her own room. As she started to get ready for the day, her mind wandered, yet again. She had an instinctive feeling that today was going to be different but couldn't quite understand how or why. She brushed her long hair before slipping into a pair of jeans and one of her favourite soft red sweaters with the slogan, '*Freedom*' in white letters written across the front. It spoke volumes to Hannah, and she felt it represented her. It could not have been more apt for the day, as she was about to begin her quest to overcome The Watchers control over The Gifted Ones.

With Amelia still in the back of her mind, she began to mentally work a few things out. There were so many questions she wished she had asked Queen Nail. Her thought process went like this:

Thoughts Number One: The Book of Spells

'Before heading off, give Amelia the Book of Spells. Tell her to keep it under her pillow. Everything can be explained when I get back from investigating The Watchers. It will be too much to go into it all now; like how it can only be used in life-or-death circumstances. Maybe that is what Queen Nail meant by 'use carefully?' Doodle also told me to keep it safe. Amelia is my sister though; surely, I can trust her? The tiny pages of the book are papyrus, wow, just like the letter was from The Belief Council.'

Thoughts Number Two: The Necklace of Belief

'Why haven't I got a necklace yet? What was the meeting date again? Should I wait for the meeting or listen to Queen Nail? No, I have the panther pendant Parky is enough. He is with me always.'

All this mindful babbling began to bring back fond memories of

Tom as well as the Battle of Minds in the summer. Apart from a few messages, she had not heard from him at all. She had been secretly hoping for a letter and not a day passed by that she had not wondered how he was getting on. Handsome, tall, athletically built, with jet black wavy hair. He would be nineteen soon. The same sensation of a flurry of butterflies danced inside her tummy. Even though his Gift had been restored, Hannah wondered if he was staying mentally strong, living among The Watchers. A flash of jealously came over her as her mind flickered to the Watcher Girls. She hoped they would not be trying to steal him from her. They all seemed very beautiful and even though they conformed to The Watcher dress code of black gypsy skirts and blouses, some did have an artistic flare, which Tom liked. She couldn't help but wonder if he was staying as valiant and honourable as she had left him.

She grabbed the Book of Spells and headed to Amelia's room. Respectfully knocking the door, tongue in cheek, she gingerly stepped in and peered around the corner. Surprised she wasn't there, she simply assumed they had arrived back and were downstairs in the kitchen. Then carefully, she placed the little book under her pillow. She would explain it to her when she got downstairs.

"A m e l i a" she yelled, stretching out the sound of her name whilst racing down the stairs.

"Not back yet H a n." Replied Tim in an equally stretched out and raised tone. He was still absorbed in his science stories with Joy. A shiver ran down her back realising it was not Amelia whom she had waved at earlier in the bedroom window.

Just then, the doorbell gave out its sharp shrill ring. It not only deafened, but also halted Hannah in her tracks. Opening the door, it was Bob the postman. “Morning. International letter, this one!” He said, ruffling in his bag, before passing it to Hannah. The cold air whipped around her feet.

“Thank-you.” she replied, retrieving the letter. Without looking up, she turned her back to the door, closing it with her foot. Poor Bob, it happened a lot. More people were interested in the mail than him, he was a chatty fella.

It was a letter from Tom!

She plonked herself on the bottom stair, skim reading it, focusing on the all-important parts.

> *‘I know it’s a bit late notice and kinda wanted to surprise you, but mom and dad have got me a ticket to visit you for our birthdays! Exciting hey? Never been to England before. Can’t wait to meet Amelia and your folks. Our birthday gifts to each other! I know you like letters so wanted to tell you this way. Message me when you get it. I have really missed you. Tom x’*

Hannah looked up at the stained-glass window at the top of the front door a little bit shocked. That was soon she thought. Her and Amelia’s birthday was November 5th and his was 14th.

She felt herself falling into a thinking frenzy, beginning to fret. A familiar intuitive feeling was beginning to develop, telling her she was needed, but how, she didn’t know. ‘Oh Tom, why now?’ she said aloud. She began to feel hugely distracted, finding reasons not to listen to what The Great Star was clearly leading her to do. A similar force was also crystalising thoughts in her mind, that today would be the day she would venture to Watcherland, where The Watchers lived. The worry caused split feelings. Was she to attend to Tom's letter or her commitment to her Gift? The loss of control, combined with all these thoughts, sparked a feeling of slight anger in her. Something a Gifted One is always looking to avoid.

Frustrated, she looked up at Mini in the portrait. 'What shall I do?' Already knowing what her answer would be. To be honourable. Of course, she knew this was right, but not what she wanted to hear. What happened then was pure 'magic Mini.'

A hazy glow wrapped a shaft of light, came diagonally down from the portrait. Hannah's power purged a beam of light from her chest and, almost instantly Mini was there, covered in a cloudy haze.

"Hannah darling, let me tell you how we are going to handle this situation. We are going to put it in a 'panther pigeonhole,' now look."

Fluttering their tiny wings, panther fairies, at least twenty as before, seemed to appear and began assembling a pigeonhole storage box right in front of her. Her pendant pulsated. Two of the panther fairies then took the letter from out of her hand and carefully placed it into one of the pigeonholes.

"There." Mini said clapping her hands together. "All safe and sound and out of mind for now. We aren't ignoring it, but sometimes we can't deal with everything all at once. Trust The Great Star, prioritise and stay focused. All will be dealt with when the time is right, and your letter will be here waiting for you. Keep believing Hannah." And winking she said, "Always together in heart."

The cloudy haze began to disperse as did the panthers, the pigeonhole, and her letter! Mini was back in the portrait. Frozen in time.

Hannah accepted the situation rather calmly. She had learnt about the negativity of controlling situations through her experience of The Watchers and Tom. *'In order to truly forgive she knew she had to surrender control.'*

Picking up her battered old pale blue sneakers that lay by the kickboard, she put them on before grabbing her navy-blue woollen peacoat that was hung in the hall, along with her red scarf, wrapping it tightly around her neck. Where she was going, she did not quite know, which was bizarre knowing her hometown so well. But that was just it, she didn't know it all. She would have to disappear to discover.

It was quite good she thought that her dad was preoccupied, and Mum was out with Amelia, she could slip away quietly, but opening the door gently who should be standing on the doorstep, Belinda, and Amelia.

"Where are you going?" Amelia blurted out.

"Morning darling." Belinda chirped in.

"I've been looking for you, I can't talk now. I have left something under your pillow, look after it for me until I return. Ok?"

Amelia pursed her lips, with a look of 'why should I?' Followed by a look of 'what is she going on about?'

Hannah gave her a pleading look, "please?"

Belinda nodded firmly at Hannah and with a gentle hand ushered Amelia into the house, "Gosh it's chilly girls." She said.

As Amelia headed off down the hall, Belinda turned to Hannah, and in a maternal voice said, *"Be careful of what you allow into your mind."* A tear welled up in her eye, she knew, just like Mini had in the summer, that Hannah's time had arrived.

Pulling the door closed behind her, she could not help thinking, if Amelia hadn't been in her room or even been in the house, what or who was it that she had seen from the garden?

She was about to find out.

Chapter Seven

Part One –A series of complications
Part Two – A Slippery Path

A Series of Complications

To Watcherland Hannah bravely wandered. To Pocklington, near where the castle stood. Her journey though held complications, fourteen in total to be precise.

As she left home, turning left, it was the wave from Mrs. Gives, standing outside Jigsaw cottage, that left her feeling disconcerted. Had Hannah not decided to turn around she would not have seen her. Odd, she thought, seeing her standing there? She was beginning to realise that anything was possible and Gifted Ones often unknowingly intertwined with each another. It did distract her initially as she made her way towards the humpback bridge, which to locals was recognisable as the entrance to Pocklington. 'Castle

Walk,' the road to the bridge itself was a rather long one and it was on this part of the journey that the first three complications occurred. Hannah and Amelia were forbidden from playing in Pocklington when they were younger. She now felt as though she was carrying not only her own nerves but also that of her twin.

'Castle Walk', aptly named for its unparallel views of the town's historic site, was certainly pleasant enough. A moss-covered red brick wall lined it, leading up to the bridge, perhaps a couple of hundred years old. It was a neat looking wall, still red in parts where the original brick colour had not faded the over the years, with rounded blocks at the top. Today, tickled from the frost, the wall glistened smoothing out the rougher bricks, giving it a much-needed youthful glow. Apart from the odd patch of graffiti, with the interspersed regal trees lining the wall, and the castle as a backdrop, it was not hard to imagine Kings and Queens strolling along in a by gone era. Hannah though was not taking the 'scenic' route today, her eyes and ears were peeled, as were The Watchers.

Suddenly out of nowhere, breaking the serene silence, a mad frenzy of cawing crows fled one of the tall trees, shaking the frost like frozen confetti to the ground. A few of the branches looser twigs broke off and the last remaining leaves of autumn floated to the ground.

The flapping of their feathers released a toxic smell, like the one she first noticed upon returning home. It was a mouldy smell like algae, enough to make her pull her red scarf over her nose. Feeling nervous, she knew The Watchers were close by, it brought back the terrifying feeling of when she first saw Victor transform into a crow. In her mind she began to visualise the huge tunnel of grey light that burst forth from his chest. She momentarily thought of the process that this kind of Watcher might take during their transformation, and in doing so quickened her pace in an ironic way, enthusiastically walking toward the possible danger she was about to encounter.

It was then that the shiny clear sky, the colour of light blue with perfectly formed clouds began to change. Becoming dull, a wave of grey rippled overhead, and it was as though the dog of the sky had shaken its muddy coat, spraying droplets and splattering the clouds. As more appeared, it became cooler leaving a dampness in the air with a heavy, billowing feeling that the sky was about to break. It was the first complication.

It was happening all over again, memories of her first journey to The Watchers neighbourhood in America came flooding back, except this was no test of Doodles, as it had been then. This was Watcher activity. Each of the many clouds began to take the shape of an eye, a piercing mean eye and they were all staring directly at Hannah.

The sky was now littered with eyes, known as Watcher clouds. In their multitude they stared, watched, and followed this favoured Gifted One. But thankfully, underneath her scarf she felt the warmth of the pendant. It was hard to continue, but the eyes were here to stay. Piercing down upon her journey, their watch wore heavy. Then, the second complication occurred. The more the eyes stared, the more her feelings of doubt grew.

'Go back home,' the trees seemed to say, their words chiming in the cool damp air. They had traded their twinkling laden leaves for austere branches, laid hauntingly bare.

The white painted cast iron sign, 'Pocklington' that stood at the bottom of the bridge, could not have appeared soon enough. It was then the third complication happened.

Whilst hurriedly walking along, she fell over something. Exactly what she couldn't tell, but she landed on her hands and knees in a giant puddle at the foot of the sign. The water, gathered from the melting frost, gained depth, and feeling it rising she was unable to feel the ground beneath her. Something slippery slithered by her legs and with her eyelids forcibly closed, she drifted into what seemed to be an unconscious state. The fourth complication quickly occurred.

The puddle had gained great depths, so too, deep in Hannah's mind something was stirring, bringing Queen Nail to life to aid her. Then coming face to face with her, Hannah's full attention was bought back. Even submerged under water, Queen Nail's crown of stars shimmered, taking on an amber glow against the greyness of the water. Her silver hair flowed gently against the slow underlying current. The rich colour of her blue velvet tunic felt comforting to a disorientated Hannah and in her gentle voice, distorted under water, she said as bubbles softly flowed out,

"It's time to believe Hannah. Do not let the doubt creep in dear; nail yourself to your belief."

Hannah understood fully what she meant.

By the power of her tail, every imaginable shade of blue, holding onto each of her arms, she thrust them both up towards the water's surface. Hannah found herself back on her hands and knees looking down into a puddle again, the face of Queen Nail below, peering back up at her. Then, slowly, she disappeared into the incomprehensible depths.

Remarkably, she was neither wet nor cold. The warmth from her glowing panther pendent had kept her dry; it was now thawing her anxiety. Before she knew it the fifth complication came.

Bending over her, offering a helping hand, she heard a man quietly mutter, "Do you need any help?"

Looking over her shoulder, still on her knees, the man of smallish stature stood hovering above her with a hand extended out. Wearing a scarf, with a black blazer over a white lab coat, which hung below his knees resembling a skirt, it was none other than Don Surlin, the chemist.

He rarely made eye contact with his customers, today though, his deep-set eyes, slightly narrowed, homed in on her as he gazed down. They resembled those of the Watcher clouds.

She noticed a tiny snake slither across his eye as she instinctively grabbed his hand, pulling her up. Shocked by what she saw, she quickly snatched her hand away. Then complication number six happened.

In a facetious way he said, "Aren't you a bit old to play in puddles? Don't you think you should head back to Ashby town, or are you going to continue to play around here?" His eyes narrowed and the tiny snake passed over his iris again, disappearing into his pupil.

The whole thing felt weird and creepy, and she could feel herself nervously perspiring. Was he a Watcher she wondered? Surely not Mr. Surlin. The damp air felt humid with the Watcher clouds still hanging heavy in precipitation.

Her pendant began pulsating as a voice inside, deep and meaningful, like Parky's said, 'I know them all. Don't trust yourself to them.' Parky's voice always soothed her, appearing just at the right time. He walked alongside her and in this instance in a confident manner she replied, "No playing for me today, Mr. Surlin" and walking a few steps towards the middle of the bridge, she casually lent against the wall as he creepily walked on by.

When he had gone, she stayed looking beyond the bridge at the homes in Pocklington before gazing down into the brook. The view from the other side of the bridge was perhaps the fairer as it looked towards the castle. The smell from the brook was pungent and it flowed at a fast pace. It was quite noisy, but the sound of the water was soothing, if only temporarily. Murky is perhaps the best way to describe the colour of the water along with dirty and dreary.

For a second time, Hannah fell as the seventh complication occurred. Out of nowhere, a multitude of fish leapt out of the water, startling her. Repetitively, they plopped back down into the brook before rising again to the height of the bridge. Some hovered with wings mid-air, staring directly at her. It was of course, the other type of Watcher, flapping, flailing, flying Watcherfish, with the body of a lizard and the face and beak of a crow.

Frightened, she cowered down behind the wall, but taunting her they jumped it, landing in front of her, before flying off again.

Putting her head in her hands she could feel her blood boiling. Anger raced through her like lightening and standing up, at the top of her voice she screamed, "NO! NO! NO!" In defiance, a swarm of them jumped up out of the water, hovering and hissing before retreating into the water. It was reminiscent of The Watcher's behaviour earlier that summer on Spyglass Hill Drive.

She was rather surprised at her steely response. This was the armour Queen Nail had mentioned, the pure strength of a Gifted One which lies deep within.

Part Two – A Slippery Path

Complication eight was far less dramatic, but still important in what was turning out to be a remarkable run of events. It occurred as Hannah bravely wandered around the outside of The Watcher's homes.

The bridge led straight onto a steep grassy bank, littered with seasonal native wetland plants. Green parallel threads brimmed the water's surface, floating like jellyfish's tentacles.

All the Watcher homes set back from the bank were carefully interspersed, at least forty to fifty, with a clear view of the brook. Hannah felt the need to wrap her scarf tightly around her neck as she strolled the bank, looking at the different homes and the grassy passageways between them. They all looked the same, cottages with heavily thatched roofs and to say they appeared dark and damp, was an understatement. Single story with a grey façade, no windows, just a front door. Letting light in physically and mentally was avoided in Watcherland. The only evidential warmth was from the grey smoke of a fire which whirled from a few chimney pots. It was eerie and not a single Watcher could be seen. Feeling vulnerable, it was her sheer determination that propelled her to be brave and continue exploring, which she did, deciding to venture up the grassy paths in between the cottages. The ground underfoot was muddy, unlike the sturdy bone-dry ground of her own frost laden garden. Her battered blue sneakers squelched.

She was pleased that none of the cottages had windows, as no one could look out, even though she felt she was being watched all the time. A little way ahead, in the distance, stood the outline of a tall woman, by what looked like a small lamppost. Hannah felt a strange feeling of fear, mixed with excitement as she walked towards her. With her nose running, she nervously began to sniff, thinking the worst that could happen would be for this woman to transform into the new type of Watcher, in front of her very eyes. Or did they need to be by the brook to do that? She recalled witnessing The Watchers transform before and simmering her thoughts she reassured herself that Parky was with her always.

Drawing closer to the figure, strangely it did not look around, nor move away. Recognising the back of the tall woman, Hannah realised it was Joy. Her tall AI body dressed in jeans and t-shirt with beautiful long hair, untied, hanging down her back. Randomly, she thought 'strange, mum always ties it back.' Thinking it not to be Joy in Watcherland, her usual overthinking began to consume her and stuttering she spluttered out, "Joy? Joy?"

As Joy turned around, what Hannah thought to be a small lamp-post behind her, was in fact her imaginary friend from the summer, Nancy the lamp, crying, blubbering, and shaking uncontrollably, it caused her to wobble.

"Nancy, Nancy, what's wrong, I thought you were...gone?" Hannah said utterly confused. Nancy had been destroyed from Hannah's imagination in the Battle of the Minds.

"Joy, what are *you* doing in Pocklington? Go home. Now!" Her authoritative armour had come into play again.

Running robotically, Joy fled, looking like a character from a police sci fi movie, firstly back to the bank of the brook before mechanically taking a sharp left as she sped off towards the bridge.

Flabbergasted, Hannah naturally tried to comfort Nancy placing an arm around her lamp and body. But she was unable to, she was ghost like.

"Nancy what's going on?"

In her distinctive drawl, she replied, "Hannah, don't you stop believing, and don't forget that Book of Spells now! *These troubles will carve your inner star to shine brighter.* There's trouble in the camp I say. These guys are worse than those crows."

Then she was gone, vanished. Even though she had not been there anyway. She had not taken in Nancy's comment of 'trouble in the camp.'

Spinning around to check where she had stopped and skidding on the mud, she noticed she was a little further down, back from the brook, at the door of one of the cottages. Sneaking around the back of this cottage, she hung back watching an older woman ushering out two young boys, around ten years old. 'Now I'm the one watching,' she thought.

"Straight to that bus stop. Get on and go to the group. Remember to keep a watch on any Gifted. Do *not* get caught up in that believing. Remember it will only disappoint you. It is *not* real." She emphasised the word not. The boys gave a firm nod and playfully skuttled off.

Quite clearly under the lady's control, Hannah wondered if the Elder Watchers, here in her hometown, abided by the 'Watcher Crowcode' as they did at her grandmothers. The boys heading to a Watcher group with school closed, would have sadly had it instilled in them from an early age not to be allured into becoming a Gifted One. So sad to be deprived of so much joy, thought Hannah.

The lady's profile was sad. Hannah was familiar with the forlorn look of a Watcher, but she seemed to recognise this lady. It was Mrs. Robinson, the fishmonger. Surprised again from the people she knew in her hometown. Widowed, Mrs. Robinson naturally had reason to be sad losing her husband, but unbeknown to Hannah, once she had been a true believer and shone as bright as a Gifted One. Upon the loss of her husband, all her light faded, at a time when The Great Star could have comforted and supported her. She became bitter, resenting the light in others, knowing hers had gone. A lifetime dressed in black both on the inside and out, her husband was not the only thing she was mourning. The women Watchers dressed not much different to their American counterparts, long black gypsy style skirts and blouses. Mrs. Robinson today, was also wearing a shawl over her shoulders. The boys, who naively had skipped of moments ago, had been attired in what you could say was a boys junior Watcher look. Black boots, knee high grey socks and shorts, with a dark blazer.

Hannah waited for Mrs. Robinson to close her door before heading back to the bank and glancing up, she could see the Watcher clouds still staring down.

Complications nine and ten happened in quick succession.

There were several rickety wooden bridges that crossed the brook, accessing the road which weaved its way out of Pocklington, back to Market Street. A logical thinker, some of the time, Hannah assessed the road ahead. Surely public transport seemed the only viable way in and out of the area?

Crossing the bridge, the two boys she had seen earlier stood chatting, showing each other tiny toy cars whilst waiting for the bus.

The Watchers saw it as an advantage mixing their young with The Gifted at school. Regularly roused by the Elders, to remain focused as Mrs. Robinson had, they saw it as an open invitation to prey. On the contrary The Gifted saw it as an opportunity to extend their belief. The Watchers were pushing pressing down whilst The Gifted were always trying to pull up.

Seeing Hannah, the boys gave her a cursory glance, before returning to their chat. As with most children, their attention span was short, and they reverted to more interesting things like the toy cars they were holding. She didn't recognise them, perhaps Mrs.

Robinson was their grandma? They were too young to attend Tower High School, maybe they were still at 'Mid Tower,' the middle grade school?

As the huge bus pulled alongside, seemingly from nowhere, it caught Hannah unaware. Twizzling around she slipped on the mud just as the aluminium beast pulled up alongside.

It must be snug for that to fit over the humpback bridge she thought, and getting up to her feet she could see the boys on the back seat waving to her. That was complication number nine.

The tenth complication was to be the most harrowing unfathomable experience of them all.

Across the road, a couple of girls were running towards the bank of the brook from the cottages. The water seemed particularly active and the aroma was now stronger, enough for the need to cover her nose with her scarf again. Frowning inquisitively, she wondered where they were going as they hopped and skipped merrily, as if it were a summers day. She could see from afar that they were her age and reaching the bank she recognised them. It was Renee and Beth from her school. They were in her and Amelia's class.

It was a defining moment for Hannah, encountering girls she personally knew, who could be Watchers. She wouldn't be surprised if they were though; Tom had said Watcher girls were all beautiful, at least on the outside, often shallow inside. Beth and Renee resembled the girls she had seen back in the summer, the ones Tom described. Their gypsy skirts were above the knee, layered, and each had long black socks, jewelled at the top with neat ankle boots.

They wore black denim jackets with a snakeskin detail over the shoulder and down the arm. They also wore quite heavy makeup and their hair hung down wild and free.

At school, Beth and Renee were terrible bully's and incredibly gossipy. These were the girls who had got Amelia in trouble. They spent their time at school huddled together sniggering, making snidey comments and wanting to be in the know of what was going on. They were suspicious of everything, set about false rumours and were constantly competing to be in the action of it all, which often happened with the aid of their alluring looks and persuasive manner. Hannah had seen through them from an early age and now felt a sense of relief maybe being able to rationalise why they were like this. In a way, she now concluded, it was not their fault they had been raised to portray themselves in this insecure manner. Both girls spotted her,

"Oh Hannah Timms, heard you were back. What are you doing here, Oh holy one! Found your Gift, have you?" Beth led the sarcastic remarks, leaving her sidekick Renee giggling.

Continuing to taunt, she said, "We will show you *our* power if you show us your panther."

"Winged panther, save me, save me!" they both said continuing to tease her, and in fits of giggles they ran side to side and up and down the bank, flapping their arms in make believe flight.

"It's the necklace we want." Renee said changing her tone seriously, folding her arms. Her tone turned to a muffled squeal. One that Hannah sadly, was only too familiar with,

were Watchers; she even saw an eel. The sunken banks were covered in submerged plants. Moss covered the rocks and weeds wafted by the current. Algae floated like jellyfish, being tossed and turned by the rapid movement of some The Watcherfish she saw.

Queen Nail, having let go of her hands, stayed protectively close by behind Hannah, as she allowed her to explore, swimming in the same motion as a dolphin. The brook seemed to stretch on for miles, becoming narrow and restricted in places. The 'Armour of light' perpetuated the space they were in and allowed them to go unnoticed.

After a little while of eavesdropping on conversations of 'Who's Watching Who,' a common slogan used by Watchers, she came across a huge shoal waiting to pass into another part of the brook, where it became divided. A natural archway made of rock separated the brook at this junction and at the top of it was a square rock plaque. Etched upon it was the image of a crown with two eyes with a snake across each.

It was her newly given ability of being able to hear underwater that would bring about the eleventh and twelfth complications, as she gained valuable information about her mission.

Queen Nail's unspoken nod, to proceed into the unknown zone of the brook, propelled Hannah forward. The moment she entered, there was absolutely no mistaking she was in an underwater 'Spectacle Council.' A rock suspended by old rotten rope hung cockeyed, with the words, 'Council Chamber.' Along the side of the bank and on the roof of the arch, were etchings of the castle and more eyes, as well as many images of winged snakes with the face and beak of a crow.

As many Watcherfish began filling the space, eleven of them swam up to the etchings on the arched rock roof and stayed for a few seconds, venerating them. As they paused, Hannah moved in closer, noticing they each wore a chained necklace with a pendant of a winged snake as depicted in the etchings. A little while later, another fish swam in to join them. Swimming to the head of the school it welcomed the others before showing adoration to the etchings. 'Maybe this was the leader of the council?' she thought to herself, but how would she be able to differentiate who the leader was? Moving in for closer observation, she saw a tiny snake slither over the Watchers eye. Startled, she flipped backwards, looking behind at Queen Nail. Quickly she swam in-between all the others, checking if their eyes featured a snake, none of them did.

Perplexed, she began to piece it all together and complication eleven became apparent. Was Mr. Surlin the leader of the underwater Spectacle Council?

"The favoured one has entered our territory. We now have the ultimate prize at our disposal, the spirit of the Panther, to destroy forever! NOW, I say, NOW, is the time to gather The Gifted together at the castle for The Great Gifted Nickolous. When we have defeated the weakest, we will attack the favoured."

Hearing the twelfth complication, Hannah fell into despair as she remembered how death consumed the sky back in the summer, as Parky's lifeless body was hauled by crows through the still, silent air. Noticing her anguish, Queen Nail began to usher her out of the council chamber.

"Enough for now, my dear." She comforted her, and they swam back unnoticed by their invisibility, to where they had first entered the brook and were propelled vertically out, the same way they had both entered. Hannah's body again was instantly restored and remarkably dry. Gently gliding her over to the bridge, Queen Nail tenderly placed her down. "See you back in the garden dear." There, she would return to a stone statue.

The thirteenth complication occurred on the bridge.

A feeling of confidence having gained a certain amount of knowledge reigned as she caught sight of her red scarf swaying gently in the breeze. It was looking tattered, having been pecked at by The Watchers. She gazed upward, noticing the eyes of the sky were slowly reappearing.

There was no way she could reach her scarf now, so she decided to sit on the wall of the bridge to wait to see if it would become dislodged. Her newfound confidence and adventurous spirit had enflamed her ego. Boldly she began to think of other Watcher areas she had not yet explored; for instance, The Flushing Meadows that Mini had told her about. The higher ground, where the waterfalls existed. In that moment Hannah's determined mind wanted to conquer it all. She even began to plot an allied approach, in a war against The Watchers, thinking of who may frequent these places and if she knew any of them, along with the Gifts she could save.

By visiting The Flushing Meadows, which she was thinking of,

Watchers hoped that dark forces controlling them could be flushed, in the expectation of a conversion. What Hannah didn't know was that Pocklington didn't have Flushing Meadows, they were in fact Flushing Waterfalls, upon the higher ground. It was here that Watchers seeking redemption would fly high out on the crest of the waterfall in the hope of attracting The Great Stars attention. As always it was only true belief that made the process possible.

It was all waiting for Hannah and for now she had resigned herself to leaving the scarf in Watcherland. 'It would be interesting to see what happens to it' she thought and headed back towards Castle Walk.

At the foot of the bridge, she looked left towards the castle. The brook flowed ahead for a while, before becoming submersed underground. Her courageous spirit led her to the fourteenth and 'Grandes' complication.

The weather changed almost immediately as she walked along the brooks bank towards the castle grounds. It was dusk and very quickly a fog had formed, making visibility difficult. Hannah knew the path and felt relieved to be back, not only on familiar territory but firmer ground, even though the air was strikingly cold, making her shiver.

Relieved, she gave a long sigh, 'phew it had been the longest day of my life,' she thought. 'As though it was never going to end.' Little did she know, *anything was possible, even the impossible, by following the path of The Star.*

Ahead, the huge castle tower had fought the fog and the familiar tooth shaped battlements were visible. She had convinced herself that it was a change to head home this way, even though it was out of the way and certainly the longer route. Before she knew it, she was in the grounds of the castle. Without realising it, Hannah was standing over the crypt, where centuries ago eggs had been laid by The Watcherguards, creating this formidable breed of Watcher.

Thoughts of her grandfather here, lying dead, flooded her mind. It was the first time she had been to the castle since she had returned home. Curiosity robbed her sorrow, remembering Mini telling her how Hunter had been found here, petrified, shattered glasses in one of his hands and a few silver coins in the other. Why was that? The fog thickened and an unnerving feeling came over her.

Rising from over the castle wall appeared nothing more than what could be described as a monster. A snake of preposterous proportions slithered itself down the long wall of the tower.

This absurd creature with the body of a snake, as dark as the night sky, and the wings of a swan, whiter than snow, with the face and beak of a crow reached the ground, swaying from side to side towards Hannah, before arrogantly raising up before her, hissing,

"Be my Queen, Hannah. Queen of the castle. Queen of my world. I will give it all to you if you surrender the panther and yourself to me."

It was the Great Gifted Nickolous. Face to face with the favoured Gifted One, tempting her.

She had walked consciously into a terrifying nightmare.

Eye to eye with this monstrosity, her pendant pulsated powerfully as Parky the Panther leapt forwards from it, landing on the ground. Standing in front of Hannah, turning to face Nickolous, Parky opened his thick white lustrous wings blocking Hannah completely from view.

The space around Parky became galactic, whilst Nickolous seemed restricted. In the shadow of his presence, Nickolous slyly slithered and coiled himself, retreating towards the tower.

"The light will ALWAYS overcome the darkness, Nickolous, and there is abundant room in it." His deep meaningful voice echoed through the cold evening air.

"NEVER! Your protection will fade and burn out, just like your Star." Hissed Nickolous.

"This is MY Kingdom!" He continued to hiss, as he slithered up the tower and over the wall.

When he was gone, Parky turned to Hannah, looking ethereal and gradually fading, proclaimed,

"With my protection you will be able pick up such a snake in your hand, and not be harmed." And he was back in the pendant. Always ready to serve all, who believed in him.

It was this mystery of faith that certainly served Hannah, but which also kept her in the wilderness of Watcherland for so long. She would have to dig deep to keep believing and trust the process because what she did not know, was that when she arrived home, Tom would be waiting for her. She was now seventeen having missed her birthday and it was early December.

Star of the Sea Church
Church Street
The Arena
Castle
Tower
Crypt
Pocklington Watchers
Castle Walk
Upper Bridge Street
Flushing Waterfalls
POCKLINGTON

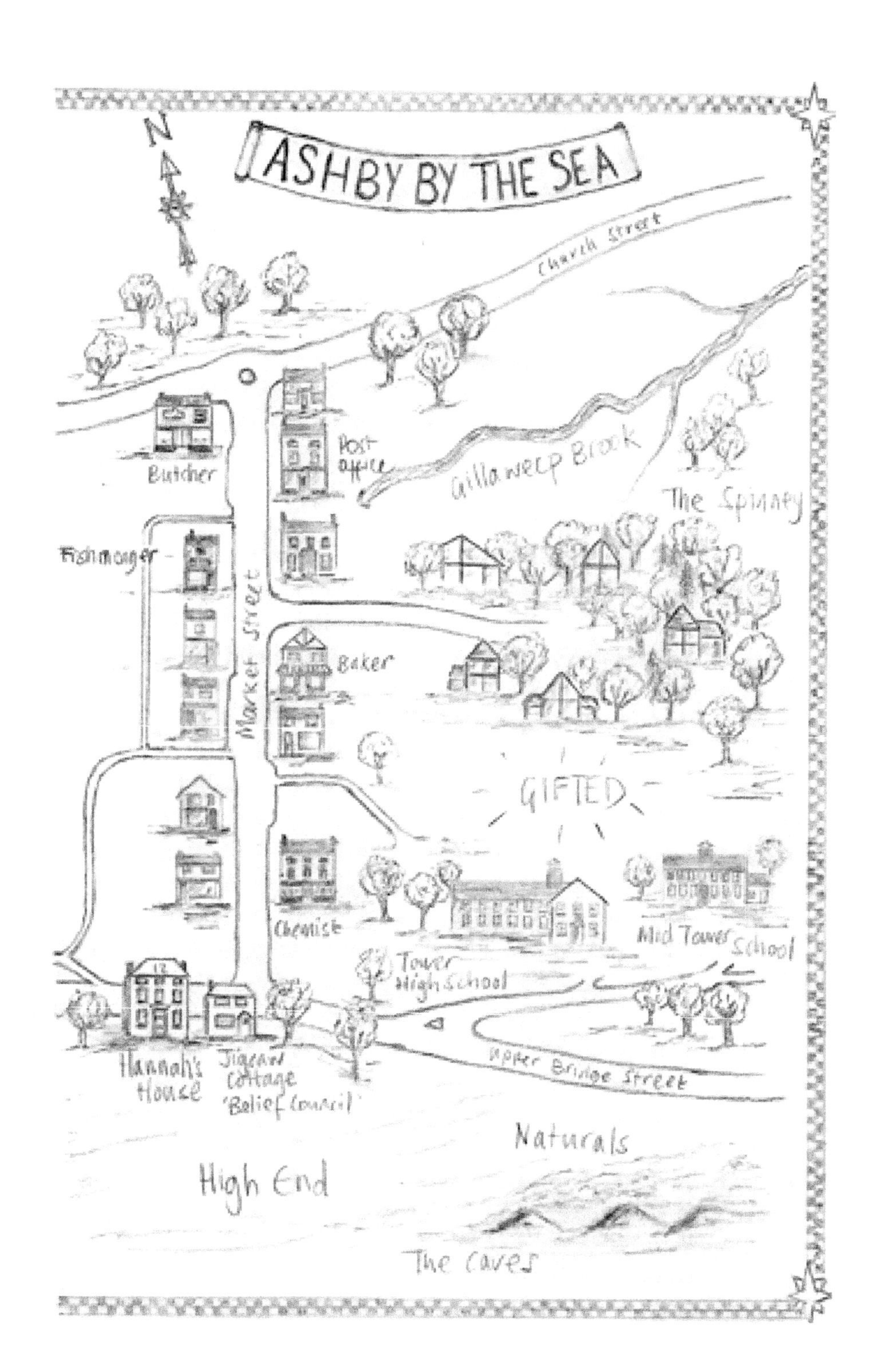
ASHBY BY THE SEA
N
Church Street
Butcher
Post office
Brook
The Spinney
Fishmonger
Market Street
Baker
GIFTED
Chemist
Mid Tower School
Tower High School
12
Upper Bridge Street
Hannah's House
Cottage
'Belief Council'
Naturals
High End
The Caves

Chapter Eight

Part One – A Record of Wrongdoings
Part Two - Where the Crow Flies

A RECORD OF WRONGDOINGS

IMAGINE IF you can, Hannah running home, with thoughts of a gigantic snake with a jet-black pointed beak slicing through the air, slithering like lightening, and closing in on her as she ran home. Only moments ago, she had encountered The Great Gifted Nickolous, who over the centuries had now evolved into an even more grotesque monster, a winged snake with the face and beak of a crow. The darkness had adapted finding new ways to invade and conquer The Gifted Ones. It made Hannah think about what kind of other Watchers worldwide may exist.

Would their habitat dictate their evolution? Would there be in the deepest part of The Amazon jungle, Watchermonkeys? With tails that coiled their victims draining the light out of them and teeth that bit into their joy, bursting their bubble? Enlightened by these thoughts during her disappearance, she had concluded (after much thought) that no matter what or how many other types of Watchers may look or transform, it didn't change what they represented. Their disguise may change, their powers may increase. They may even find new ways of manipulating The Gifted and so on. But all that remains is that *'the light will always find its way through the dark.'* The Gifted only evolved spiritually.

Making it home, she found the black heavily studded front door, ajar. Breathless with heart pounding, she scampered inside, slammed the door shut and slumped onto the floor with her back up against it. Sitting forwards, with her arms resting upon her knees, her head between her legs, she took a few long breaths. In through the nostrils and out through the mouth. Slow, controlled deep breaths. Gradually the erratic breathing was more under control, and she stood up on the highly polished black and white tiled floor. On the second more controlled breath, having got herself somewhat together, she began to wonder that when she had scampered in, why a Christmas wreath was hanging on the outside of the door. It had flapped up and crashed back down, ringing its tiny bells, when she had slammed it shut. Just then, a strange feeling engulfed her, an overwhelming sense of having lost track of time. What sounded like a choral of angel's voices came from out of the black and white diamond floor tiles. Tones of the white tiles were different to those of the black, but together as their angelic voices echoed, it was heavenly. Just as they had at Mini's in the summer, the tiles began undulating to the vocal paradise. They sang, ***'It's time.'***

'Time, time, time boldly and bravely marches on.
Time is the master of presents, granting the brightest gifts.
Time you create balance, oh nature clinging to its ticking.
Time boasts perfection, be patient, you will see the beauty of its perfect timing.
It is the timing of The Great Star, Oh Star, Oh Star, Oh Star!'

Hannah was swept away by the sweet sounds of what was another astounding unfathomable experience and it soothed her from The Great Gifted Nickolous trauma. During the 'tiles time' a couple of other things had been happening. The moment she had walked through the door, 'magic Mini' had come to life. Whilst focusing on her breathing she had noticed the hazy light casting down upon the tiles before the choir had started. Now, looking up at the painting, Mini, without Hannah's imagination coming to life had appeared, looking tearful.

"Mini, what is it, you ok? Did you hear them? The angelic tiles?"

Out of the corner of her eye whilst talking, she could see the banister was wrapped in a festive garland. The light from Mini's gifted energy reflected on the copper sprayed pinecones making them appear golden. Being a three-storey house, the family garland was huge, bought out each year and wrapped around the banister, from the top of the house to the bottom. Each year Belinda would add a new creative touch to it. Last year's addition were tiny red berries scattered amongst the greenery of the artificial pine.

Again, side-tracked Hannah wondered if it was a bit early for the garland to be up.

Mini tearily began to speak, "Hannah darling, you must follow Queen Nails last instruction to meet her back in the garden. Go, right now, before you stir the house. You are entering a storm, but not the eye, not quite yet. Trust in The Star, keep believing and listen carefully."

Doing everything in her power to support Hannah, she faded away. Mini loved the girls as her own and like many mothers she wanted to take away the pain she knew awaited Hannah, but that was not possible. Being Gifted came with a profound acknowledgment of always trusting and believing. *Keeping the door to the mind and heart open.*

The cuckoo clock struck midnight. Hannah did exactly what Mini said and crept through to the kitchen and outside into the back yard. Creeping around felt odd, surely someone would have heard the front door slam shut? And what about the angelic tiles? She wasn't the only Gifted One in the house, would Amelia or mum have heard them? It was reminiscent of her return home as her pendant glowed, pulsated and a familiar unknown force quickened her step, halted her thoughts as she stood before Queen Nail. As the tunnel of light projected from the middle of her chest, Hannah felt like a small wooden boat with a beam, peddling upon the dark still ocean, being drawn into the moon light.

The yard's huge Victorian lamp light, disguised in part from the fog, gave an amber glow. The garden wall barricaded much of the blinding mist that had been created, and with the fog adding to her mystical appearance, Queen Nail, looked divine as she gloriously hovered under a crown of stars. Hannah found herself feeling secure and spellbound by her beauty. It was not just her physical beauty; it was the steadfastness she provided, as she once again was about to provide an 'Armour of Light.' The same steadfastness shone from Mini and Belinda, but this was another maternal level.

"My dear, you may have begun to feel time has been hidden from you. But nothing is lost that cannot be found, and now is the time for you to find out what took place during your disappearance. To aid you, you have been granted the gift of protection from the Armour of Light and I will remain in your imagination. My stars will shine to conceal and protect your Gifted energy but come the dawn you will once again be visible. Now go!"

Hannah listened attentively. She was an honourable young woman, even more so since she had discovered her Gift, but what she could not quite understand was why the Armour of Light was needed in the security of her own home with her family? Nevertheless, accepting the situation she trotted back inside with an air of secrecy and expectation.

As she walked invisibly into the kitchen, who should she see but Tom, standing at the fridge, casually drinking a glass of milk. Seeing him made her jump and hunching her shoulders she nervously looked around. Of course, he had not seen her. No one could see her, shrouded by an unfathomable light. He wore a white t-shirt over striped navy and white long pyjama bottoms, they looked like a pair of Tim's. The sensation of a flurry of butterflies stirred deep within her as she ogled at him. It was so good to see him! Being tall and athletically built, the tight t-shirt cut around the muscular part of his chest. Tilting his head back he swilled the last part of the milk, as though quenching his thirst on a hot summer day. Purposely placing the glass down, he leaned over the kitchen sink, resting both hands on its cold ceramic form, then lowering his head, he took a long deep breath. Hannah felt invisibly prisoned, angrily she wanted to scratch and crawl her way out of the incomprehensible protection like a cat entangled in metres of yarn wool. She was desperate to walk over and hug him, but for reasons not yet revealed, she could not.

Above the sink was a shelf and on it stood a wooden block calendar. Inscribed upon it were the words, *'Every day is a day of light.'* It was her mothers. Belinda religiously every day, turned the blocks over. The entire family gravitated around it as a way of knowing the date.

It was past midnight. Tom turned the date. It read December 5th.

"Come back Hannah. I need you." He said to the calendar. Tom had arrived as his letter had indicated.

An ice-cold feeling forming deep within her spread its icicle's far and wide into every ounce of her being, Tom, the date, her birthday. It was information overload. She felt her brain was about to explode, but The Star never gives The Gifted Ones more than they can handle. Her pendant thawed the internal ice that raged within.

Sitting down at the table, putting his head in his hands, Tom ruffled his jet-black wavy hair and banged his clenched fists upon the wooden table, staring ahead he growled angrily. His mental health, having come so far, was under pressure. 'Haven't I been through enough?' he thought. 'How can she do this to me? This wasn't how it was supposed to be. She knew I was coming. Is this her revenge from when I let her down in the summer?' Self-loathing swamped him turning quickly into anger for thinking bad things. Looking straight ahead in the direction of Hannah, his deep chocolate eyes seemed to pierce through her, making her shiver. He got up from the table and headed into the hall and up the stairs. Following him, she wondered where he was sleeping.

At the top of the house, opposite Tim's attic room, was another tiny room. It was more akin to an actual 'attic' room than Tim's larger space, but the family described it as a junk come spare room. It housed many things such as old school photos, books, and a dressing up box. The girls would madly run to the top of the house when they were little and delve into it. It was these dressing up days that were probably the catalyst for Amelia's fashion interest. It also included Belinda's painting and craft items, along with a sewing machine and luggage. A few of her paintings at one end were propped up against the wall on dust sheets, her most recent of Cork being among them. It was hard to make out the painting in the dark but, in the moonlight, sneaking through the curtain, his antlers looked magnificent. Clearly from one of Belinda's imaginative experiences as the antlers seemed to extend beyond those of a normal sized stag.

Under the window, with a clear view of the castle was a small single bed. It had a patchwork quilt on it that Belinda had made the girls many moons ago, every other patch displayed a fairy-tale scene. The room held a strange smell which could only be described as old meets new, the leather from old luggage, the paints, the lack of fresh air combined with a metal aroma that randomly drifted from Tim's room.

Tom flopped onto the bed, nestled down, and drifted off to sleep. Hannah stood in the darkness watching him. The moonlight graced his face making his pale skin translucent. It was funny seeing a strong strapping young man like Tom nestled under their old girly quilt. A mixture of emotions such as confusion and sadness for him only made her feel more helpless. All she wanted to do was snuggle up to him, have the invisibility disappear, and see him smile and eyes shine when he recognised her. It wasn't going to happen, so she decided to head to her room.

On the way down she looked over to Tim's room where Joy, sat on the chair, was charging. The gentle sound of her battery whirred, and the door was wide open, which was odd, as it was always closed for safety reasons. As she glanced over, Joy, robotically lent around and turning her head, peered out of the door towards Hannah. It was unnerving as she seemed to stare right through her, in the direction of the pendent. It made her skuttle down a flight of stairs to her bedroom, and in the background, she could hear the faint sound of cuckoo clock chiming from the dining room; it was 1am. One whole hour had passed since her arrival and unsure of the quest in hand, she panicked, knowing she only had until dawn.

Running straight over to her bed, she knelt up to peer out of the window. Queen Nail, intertwined with Hannah's thought process stood regal, her stars shining bright like a statue of liberty, lovingly, she returned her gaze.

Hannah began to think about the Book of Spells and felt the urge to retrieve it from Amelia's room. Flopping back onto the bed she felt something, the tiny book had been waiting for her. In the darkness of her room the golden clasp began glistening, beckoning her to open it, just as it had in the summer. A reminder that when trust is placed in The Star all things are possible.

Surely this was not a life-or-death circumstance though. 'Use carefully' spoke an inner voice as Hannah shuffled herself up against the bed head to slowly open it, revealing the tiny papyrus pages. Each page from the book revealed moving pictures, a film. The entire book had recorded and captured all the important events during her disappearance.

She sat, mouth agape, bewildered once again, as she carefully flicked through the entire book. As she did, the moving images emerged from the page appearing as holograms in front of her, allowing her to see the action more clearly. The book had intervened in the most magical unfathomable way, and there was only one theatre ticket for this show, and that had been reserved for Hannah.

Part two - Where the Crow Flies

The book began with Tom's arrival. Dropping his bags upon the black and white tiles, with a look of disappoint and confusion when

Belinda explained that Hannah would be gone for 'some time.' She could also see Amelia's confused, envious expression.

The book revealed only what Hannah needed to see. So, when Tom met Amelia, the moving picture zoomed in on Amelia flicking her mass of red hair and acting rather coy. When Tim shook hands with Tom, he appeared full of pride, whispering to Belinda, 'what a lovely young chap, so pleased for Hannah.'

During mealtimes, a place for lively discussions, Hannah learnt that Margaret and Richard Keys, Tom's parents, once Watchers, were at last Gifted Ones. If all went well with Tom, she thought smiling, she hoped to meet them when she visited Mini again.

Although the Gifted had triumphed overall in the summer at the Battle of Minds, there was still work to be done. When Tom mentioned he had not seen much of Victor and was unsure of his whereabouts, even though he had knowledge of him moving from Spyglass Hill Drive, it was only Belinda who the book focused on. She sat tight lipped; Hannah could sense her mother knew something about Victor.

On the same page the picture moved to Tim. In a mystified manner he listened intensely to Tom. Hannah could see him absorbing information the same way he soaked up scientific detail. She had never witnessed this intrigue in him before when they spoke about their Gifts, was it because Tom was a man talking about his Gift? Did that somehow make it more credible? She hoped not! Her father had never differentiated before.

When a scene ended, the page went blank as a prompt to be

turned. The next page would be her Birthday, their Birthdays. November 5th. Belinda and Tim always made a big deal of the girl's birthdays. Pouring time and energy in to the 'special girls.'

'One special day for two special girls.' Was Tim's mantra which usually started to be said from around early November. This year though it was a sombre affair, and the picture revealed a more restrained ambience. A candle lit cake gave more of a memorial feel than a birthday, as two lonely flames waned in the darkness of the kitchen. From the picture, it was clear that Tom and Tim seemed most perplexed. Tom was in the infancy of his Gift and struggling to understand why Hannah was not at home. It would prove to be a huge test for him.

Blowing out the candles, as the smoke spiralled to the ceiling, Amelia loving the limelight, gave everyone a hug and Joy played 'Happy Birthday' from her inbuilt music catalogue.

"Remember the light will overcome the darkness and The Star will provide," said Belinda, rather bravely, in her smoky voice with a tear in her eye, echoing the words of Mini. Focusing in on Tim, Hannah could see the frown across his forehead as he nervously ruffled his hair. His expression was a mix of anger and frustration. He had tolerated the girls' Gifts, but the worry of Hannah's disappearance was beyond measure. He directed his anger towards Belinda giving her a mean look. Not knowing their daughter's whereabouts, was probably one of the biggest challenges the family would face. Their faith would be rewarded in the eternal sphere of time and space. Even though this moment was engulfed in despair, it would fade into lesser significance in the great scheme of matters.

As she looked through The Book of Spells, the individual strobes of light outside, from Queen Nail's crown of stars, pierced through the patches of fog. It was reminiscent of a laser light display. The security of Queen Nail in her peripheral vision, along with the pendent around her neck warmed her spirit, strengthening her courage. She would need it for the next page of the book, the family decorating the house for Christmas.

Without a doubt, in most families a treasured time, Christmas in the Timms household was no different. Each person having their own specific role or job, Hannah watched as her father, with the help of Tom, dragged the Christmas conifer, wrapped tightly in mesh, across the black and white tiled floor. Hannah recalled how the smell of pine brought the great outdoors inside, the festive tree was home for the season, and she could smell it now from her bedroom.

The picture moved onto Belinda in the kitchen, wrestling with several decorative boxes. No ornament escaped her festive touch at Christmas. She was humming to the classic Christmas melodies reverberating from Joy. Her face somewhat strained, she was trying hard to keep things together and as normal as possible.

The book switched into fast forward mode, moving quickly over much of the action, including the all-important placing the tree in the same position as in previous years. Stopping, before resuming play, it paused on Amelia and Tom helping Belinda to hang the tree ornaments. This image evoked a feeling of jealousy in Hannah, as Amelia passed Tom a unicorn ornament, with a Christmas wreath around its neck, to hang from the tree. It was Toms look to Amelia that said it all. She had seen the look before, the look of love.

During his stay Tom had got to know and like Amelia and was fighting the feeling of falling in love with her. Doubt was shrouding his self-worth, bringing back old nervous feelings. His emotions for her were making him feel unworthy of being Gifted, leaving him insecure, with a desire to over control situations. The Watchers were prancing on the dark aspects of his and Amelia's feelings. Tom was being drawn into Amelia's natural insecurities, caused by the darkness she was unknowingly developing. The Watchers were cunningly feeding doubt into her, highlighting her own weaknesses whilst she lured Tom with her attractive traits, her intelligence, conscientiousness in all her achievements and, like the Watcher girls, sense of fashion and creativity.

On the next page of the tiny Book of Spells, Tom was standing in the yard wearing his favourite black leather jacket. It looked like a 'flying jacket' with the exposed sheepskin lining. It was nighttime and in the light of the garden lamp, rather arrogantly he was shaking his unicorn keyring, tempting an excited Amelia, who was dressed more like a Watcher girl in a short black skirt, long socks, and a fluffy pink jacket. They were about to share a mindful experience, and it crushed Hannah to watch.

It reminded her of the time Tom had taken her flying, as his power had enabled him to become a huge prehistoric looking bird called Hawk, named after his motorbike. Their joint gratitude then had deepened their faith and gifts as she soared upon his back on that hot summer's day. Now, she watched as the huge tunnel of light from her sister and Tom poured from their chests, bringing their imaginations to life.

The picture in the book moved to Queen Nail's troubled and concerned face. Hannah wanted to put the book down witnessing her sister and Tom together, to give in, as opposed to looking, learning, and seeking the truth. She peered at Queen Nail, returning her forlorn glance. The Queen nodded with an affirmation to proceed and continue with the rest of the book, which reluctantly she did.

On the next page, Tom's imagination had brought his unicorn keyring to life, as an imposing hologram. Pure white hair and feathers, with a long glistening horn, made the winged unicorn a magnificent creature to behold. The picture moved to Amelia standing with her imaginary friend Joy, the Amazonian warrior. Looking formidable, her long black hair and skirt rippled in the wind created by the unicorn as it was playfully prancing, swishing its tail.

Tom, having already mounted the unicorn, extended his hand to Amelia to do the same. Hannah looked on sadly; the book zoomed in on Tom's eye contact with Amelia. Greedy eyes laced with a boastful pride that even he one day would say he did not recognise. The book did not reveal Amelia's eye contact with him.

Leapfrogging from behind, Joy athletically mounted the horse, slapping its backside and within seconds they were all airborne. The moving frame reverted to Queen Nail, her stars shining.

Turning the page, a crow could be seen purposefully bombing

the unicorn's flight path, flying in front, trying to steer the unicorn of course. Hannah could see they were flying towards Pocklington. Pointing to a change of direction, towards the castle, Tom tried to divert the menace. Like a silent movie, the book played on, and Hannah watched them both smiling and flying high in the path of a clear moon. As the idyllic scene faded, the next page featured a clear view of Amelia's flaming red hair. The same tiny lizard creatures, no larger than the size of a bee, like moths to a flame, were flying around her head.

Panning to the back of the unicorn, the book focused on Joy's face. Tom and Amelia were oblivious of her face turning into Victors. It was the hissing sound and a shrill 'NEVER!' that caused him to turn around. Seeing Victors face made him tip sideways in fright, almost losing his imagination and nearly falling off, but gripping the unicorn between his legs and grabbing Amelia's hand he peeled himself back up.

Having truly believed, and thus being rewarded imaginary powers as Gifted Ones, this was now a fight to ironically eliminate it, as The Watchers were invading and doing all in their power to obstruct it and destroy it.

Hannah watched on; this was an edge of seat theatre ticket. Was Joy infected by The Watchers or was Amelia's infection causing her to corrupt her imaginative friend? If so, this would make sense why she had seen Joy in Pocklington. She felt the urge to wake her dad and get him to disconnect the family AI, to stop her working once and for all, but before her feelings devoured her, she quickly turned the next page.

Next, Joy's snake bracelets became the focus. Unbeknown to Tom and Amelia the bracelets were turning into real snakes, rapidly gaining size, strength, and length. Coiling at one end around Joy's arm for leverage, they slithered through the night air towards the front of the unicorn. Then, acting as ropes they forcibly dragged the winged beauty through the air, dragging it in the direction of the castle. Seeing them and turning to Joy, Amelia screamed. Hannah watched the fear in her sister's face, she recognised it having experienced the same fear with The Watchers herself. She could tell from Amelia's face that her sister was not imagining Joy's snakes, and still the tiny creatures flew around her head. They were almost above the castle now, as their imaginary friends faded.

Hannah turned the tiny papyrus page in haste making the paper rustle. Amelia and Tom were sitting stunned on the grass in the castle grounds. It was beyond doubt that their imaginations had faded through fear. Relief, mixed with sadness washed over Hannah as their faces revealed a terror, like her own when she had seen The Great Gifted Nickolous.

The picture paused here, as a whole host of emotions began to wash over her. The overriding emotion was jealously. Even though she could see Tom and Amelia were in trouble and something clearly wrong, this green-eyed emotional monster crawled over her, licking its lips, and spreading its tentacles. This intense feeling quickly turned to sorrow, temporarily smoothing it away, before leaving her with the worst feeling of all, that of betrayal. Yes, the one that arrogantly strips the sufferer before hanging its victim out to dry. The feeling of betrayal was brutal. Deep down Hannah's worst fear was Tom falling in love with somebody else, but surely not her sister.

The next page of The Book of Spells temporarily put Hannah's mind to rest, but at the same time worried her. A hologram appeared of Amelia sitting at her desk. Confused, looking out of the window towards the castle she was twirling her red hair. Deep in thought, displaying quite a different mood to the flicking hair habit, in front of her, opened, was The Book of Spells that Hannah had trustingly left her. What happened next was even more remarkable than Hannah could ever have imagined, but as she was learning, when The Star set a task for The Gifted, nothing got in its way. For what Amelia was thinking in that moment in time, in front of her, became displayed on the tiny papyrus pages of the book. Her thoughts were as follows.

'Why did you leave me this stupid little book Han, wonder where she is? How am I going to tell her about Tom? I like him, but I don't love him. He's good looking though. Why do I keep getting these thoughts to tell him I like him, when I don't really? I don't love him, but kind of have feelings, like fake feelings. I feel weird. He is good looking though. I wish I had a boyfriend. Why is it Han gets a boyfriend before me? She's not exactly cool looking and dresses a bit weird. Why did she get that pendant of a panther and why do I keep getting thoughts of wanting to take it? Wish I had gone to Mini's, I did like being with Mum though when she was away. I am worried about Joy.

Is she infected by The Watchers? Will they come and get me? I feel a bit scared. What about Dad? I think I'll leave this book on Hannah's bed. Shall I tell Mum?

The cuckoo clock sounded 5 am and the picture faded. Overnight the fog had cleared, and a sapphire blue sky met the dawn chorus. In the changed light, Queen Nails stars took on a golden glow. In just one hour the 'Armour of Light' would disappear and personal challenges lay ahead. Getting wrapped up momentarily in her own despondency, Hannah maturely reflected, recalling Mini's letter of getting caught up in earths desires and needs. She flipped carefully through the book; a hologram tried to pop up from one page. Opening it would define her path ahead.

It was Joy standing in Watcherland, Pocklington. A statuesque and rather imposing figure from the back, Hannah could see there was someone in front of her. A long multi-coloured scarf flicked by Joy's side and Hannah wondered why something so colourful would be in Pocklington. Panning around, the picture revealed the colourful wearer was no other than Mrs. Cox. Looking at the hologram, even though she felt incredibly tired, Hannah's eyes almost popped out of her head. 'What? Mrs. Cox is a Gifted One and the Vicar of 'Star of the Sea.' What was she doing in Pocklington with Joy?'

Looking incredibly suspicious, as the picture faded, Mrs. Cox looking over each shoulder, quickly hurried away. Without having to turn the page Joy re-emerged and this time the hologram had audio. In horror Hannah listened as Joy replayed their family conversation they had in the kitchen, about the Belief Council. What was not revealed was who she was being playing it to.

Nancy the lamp had warned her that there was 'trouble in the camp'.

As the 'Armour of Light' came to an end, Hannah slipped the Book of Spells under her pillow and as she did, she felt a piece of paper. Pulling it out, it was Tom's letter. Mini was right, the letter would be waiting for her, as was Tom.

Chapter Nine

Gathering in the Wings of Love

"DIG DEEP, *to keep believing Hannah.*"

Parky's voice had stirred Hannah's slumber, rousing her from the cusp of her dream. The low winter sun breaking through the bedroom window stroked her back with its warm rays. In the dream she was at Mini's, sitting beside Parky on the shelf. One of his wings had hung limp over the edge of the shelf, the other wrapped tenderly around her. Resting her head upon his shoulder the two friends had sat confiding in each other.

"Now that you bear the gift of belief Hannah, the darkness of doubt will make every effort to drain it away." He'd said it nobly, whilst staring straight ahead as a way of emphasising its importance, before turning back to look at her. Their blue eyes reconnecting, *"This is The Watchers game."* said Parky.

"Hannah, Han, wake up, wake up, your home!"

A spindly hand was violently shaking her shoulder, rocking her. For a moment, the perception of her dream became extremely muddled as she dozed into another one, having left the part where she was sitting with Parky upon the shelf at Mini's. Now, she was lying flat in a wooden boat on the Gillaweep brook in Ashby. Flying Watcherfish resembling underwater pallbearers were steering the boat and like a water crib she was being transported, swaying, and rocking whilst the waves, like liquid mountains, rose and fell around her. The turbulent waters she was experiencing in this part of her dream were not those from the brook, these waters stretched out like a coarse wet slippery carpet into a much wider water source.

It was a dream like prophecy which would someday fulfil the myth that a boat transported The Great Gifted Nickolous, in his casket, among the waterways. She was really getting into the thick of the action now, in all kinds of mysterious ways.

It was the sweet smell of hot chocolate, combined with the rising steam filling her nostrils, that awoke her senses fully, as she unwillingly and blurrily awakened. With her bedroom door wide open, the smell of pine had also gathered momentum and a festively dressed Amelia, in a sweater of sequins in the shape of a Christmas tree, sat on the edge of her bed. A warm glow wrapped Hannah's heart seeing her, before the realisation crept in of what The Book of Spells had revealed.

"He's here you know. Tom has arrived! Where have you been? Are you ok?"

Taking the hot chocolate from her, she shuffled to sit upright.

"Thanks."

Her mouth felt dry and blowing away the rising steam from the festive mug, she took a sip. Staring at Amelia, she sighed. She was happy to be home with her sister sitting on the edge of her bed as she so often did, especially when she wanted to share something or blurt something randomly out. It would often be early in the morning when Amelia visited her room or when they shared rooms, sat on her bed. Amelia was often to focused to lie around in bed, whilst Hannah often liked to wake and reflect. Confused, all these feelings whirled around and looking down noticed she was still wearing the 'Freedom' T-shirt from all those weeks ago.

Both sat in silence for at least thirty seconds, like when she had arrived home after the summer. Much was thought and much unsaid.

Hannah continued to blow the steam, taking sips of hot chocolate.

Flicking her hair, frowning, and looking confused, Amelia also had feelings whirling around. Constant thoughts of Hannah's pendant as well a sense of shame about Tom.

Hearing a herd of footsteps clambering up the stairs, before the pair had chance to converse, Belinda, Tim and Tom all stood in the doorway of her bedroom with Tom standing at the back.

"Hello my darling."

Belinda, teary eyed, went straight over to Hannah, flinging her arms round her, just like Amelia did when she was needy. Belinda's clinginess held high hopes upon the journey Hannah had so far taken. This vulnerability so much like Amelia's made Hannah view her mother differently. She was like Mini, yet more controlled and this openness sparked a connection of reversed roles not felt or seen before.

Next, Tim walked over to the other side of the bed, ruffling the top of her hair, he also had a tear in his eye. "Only had one special girl for a special day this year Han. Happy Birthday. So pleased your home. Good trip?"

His latter remark was laced in sarcasm, as was his sense of humour, and Hannah raised her eyebrows. Deep down he was beyond relieved with a sense of gratitude not felt before.

Tom had now moved into the room and was stood at the foot of the bed.

"Hey! Boy, am I happy to see you at long last!" He had a similar look to Amelia, with a sense of nervousness about him, which Hannah had recognised before.

Feeling as a patient might in a hospital bed, she watched as all the visitors grinned at each other, the situation becoming strangely awkward. Amelia looked behind at Tom, and then in a sulky fashion sunk her gaze back to the ground.

"I know! I will go and make a 'homecoming' lunch!" Belinda chirped in, sensing the tension. Just as Mini would clap and make tea, she used her culinary skills to bind the family.

It was now late morning. "How about a festive hotpot, something warming." Are you going to light a fire, Tim?" Being the captain of the 'home ship' everyone leaned to her instruction and went about their business.

Hannah's pendant began pulsating. The winter sun was approaching midday and its long, narrow rays shone through the window directly onto her necklace, making the copper of the panther glow intensely. Just as Belinda was about to go, everybody, even Tim, could see what was happening. Tom to date though had not witnessed the power of the pendant. The Star, transcending all beliefs was *'Shining upon those that Shine'*. It was an *'I am' moment. 'I am here.'* All the Gifted in the room felt their energies rise and without using their own Gifted imaginations, their imaginative friends stood alongside each of them, displaying their own unique powers. It was as though Hannah, from her bed, was the commander in chief inspecting an imaginative and mindful army. However, only Hannah on this occasion was able to witness everyone else's imaginary friends.

On the right-hand side of the bed stood Belinda with Cork; the huge, magnificent beast snorted. His muscular body balanced upon four fine pins had hooves that shone like freshly fitted shoes from a farrier. His antlers, already like solid branches of oak, began to gain length. Space was not an issue in Hannah's room. As before, all dimensions of space were lost. Both antlers developed razor sharp ends, and from the main trunk of each grew new, mini antlers, establishing their own penetrable sword like ends. His head bore the sword of the spirit.

"I can pierce through the doubt of The Gifted and the imagination of The Watchers." He said, intermittently coughing as seemed to be his manner. His eyes were so incredibly piercing.

Next up was Joy, the beautiful Amazonian warrior. It was not surprising for Hannah, following what was revealed in The Book of Spells, to see that her power consisted of using her snake bracelets. It was the power in her long black hair that was most surprising. Much thicker, longer, and silkier than normal, she was able to weave her hair into large nets, which she demonstrated by swishing her head, casting her hair into the infinite space, "I can make nets to catch Flying Watcherfish." She said in an animated way, because in Amelia's imagination, Joy's voice was quite high pitched. The serpents around her arms, slithered into space, gaining length and strength, how wise the tiny Book of Spells had pre-empted their power. Suddenly, something red started to appear wrapped around Joy's neck, it was Hannah's red scarf.

Some of the imaginative friends were laced in darkness, displaying areas of doubt in their believer's Gift. Hannah was about to see such darkness in Tom's unicorn, standing at the foot of her bed. Its pure white hair speckled with doubt filled black feathers, created a salt and pepper appearance, sometimes appearing blacker, then whiter, and vice versa. With its incredibly long horn, the unicorn had reluctantly begun life more akin to a moody stallion with a jet-black body and thick wings of a relatively short span. However, as Tom's Gift was restored so was the glory of his imaginative friend, just as The Star had intended.

Now, in the vastness of space it snorted and occasionally

stomped, displaying its unique power. Tom's weaknesses were the unicorns' strengths, changing size and colour. It could shrink to the size of a keyring and conceal itself in the darkness. When it spoke, Hannah was surprised by its gentle voice. She had expected a more authoritative horse tone when it said, "The ability to be seen and not seen, in size and colour, should not distract from who I am, which is to be a witness to the light." With those poignant words, the unicorn disappeared into the enormity of space, shrinking to the size of a keyring.

"Hello dear." Recognising Queen Nail's voice, she looked to where the voice was coming from, somewhere above her. Queen Nail did not need any greater power, thought Hannah, but she did, and it lay in her hands. Significant in many ways; to guide, feed, and place. Her tail above wafted; to look at her, she could have been in an ocean's deepest darkest depths, her crown of stars shone bright, made even more so by the gigantic rays stretching into oblivion. Pointing her hands downwards and splaying her fingers, she revealed long blue nails. Each nail became fortified, some of steel and some concrete and their colour changed from blue to a dazzling white.

"My nails can defend and shield, but above all, if truly desired, they can also cleanse my dear."

Queen Nail bought the unfathomable experience to a close with each imaginative friend absorbed into the space.

Tim, enlightened, instead of heading off to his room, decided to linger. The Star had instilled provoking thoughts into him which had begun to worry him. He was beginning to feel ashamed of even considering believing in anything 'unfathomable.' Science after all was in his blood.

Hannah watched, his eyes were glazed, he held the exact same look, gazing up after reading an interesting article or whilst listening to Joy recite some science from her audible library.

That night as she headed to the top floor to chat with Tom and spend some time alone with him, her dad's situation became apparent to her. Poking her head around his door, she nosily checked if he was in his room. There, she saw a couple of books sitting on his chair. Nothing out of the normal, except for the titles… 'The Truth in Unfathomable Belief' and 'A Hermits Life'

Not your average science read.

Chapter Ten

Christmas Clarity

A fair few days had passed, and Advent for many, was now in full swing. Belinda, unable to control events, busied herself ensuring Christmas would 'carry on as normal.' Calendars stuffed with chocolates and tokens were joyously opened each morning, cards were lovingly being made and amidst much baking, the evenings consisted of watching festive films. It was a useful distraction as tension between The Watchers and The Gifted Ones had intensified. Tom, having liaised with his parents, explained the situation with The Watchers in Ashby by the Sea and it was agreed he could extend his trip throughout the festive holidays. Even though his parents, Richard and Margaret Keys, had moved neighbourhoods, any kind of news always spread quickly among The Watchers, feeding their thirst for gossip, and verifying their slogan, 'Who's Watching Who'. Following the Battle of Minds that Summer, not all

The Watchers around where Mini lived had been converted. Despite the instability, Tom wanted to stay with Hannah to address his own developing insecurities and genuinely heal their relationship. She had confided and spoken in depth with in him about The Book of Spells, feeling it was important that she stood by him in times of trouble. In part, she felt it was not his fault that he was infected by The Watchers curse, the virus of the mind, however, as she had learnt during the summer, Tom was prone to lack in self-confidence and courage. Some of the Gifted needed constant pruning. Hannah knew that their love had grown out of adversity. She was also learning that The Star placed people in each other's paths at the perfect time. Together they were better.

Somehow too, Hannah seemed more intrinsically linked to her mother and Mini. They were like the three amigos, nothing slipped out of the net and were all so spiritually close, yet Hannah had not disclosed to her mother what The Book of Spells had shown her, she didn't feel the need to do so and followed her own spiritual intuition.

Watching things unfurl and relationships develop, had caused Amelia to grow sulkier and broodier by the hour; Joy had also become increasingly obsessed with Hannah's pendant. Belinda had spoken to Tim about the idea of perhaps letting Joy have a vacation, and 'disconnect' over the holidays. She had concerns that she may have been amongst The Watchers. Tim though, seemed preoccupied and detached, having gone into 'thinking' overdrive and felt she was not getting anywhere with their discussion. Learning a date had been set for Hannah to join the Belief Council was good news. Hannah missed her inauguration, so a special meeting had been convened. In her absence, the council's initial restrictions had been lifted. She would now be able to share the experiences during her disappearance with not only Belinda, but also Mrs. Gives and the Leader of the council, Ann.

The Gifted Ones, like chess pieces, placed so very carefully. Precise as time itself, as clear as Black and white.

Hannah, like her father had developed a mantra, repeating Parky's words, *'dig deep to keep believing.'* So it was with an extra squeeze that Hannah held tightly onto Tom's hand, in hope, and maybe a little hopelessness, as they walked together down Market Street. Supporting one another at the right time, they worked well as a couple.

The sky was a creamy grey colour, full of snow and cold enough to disguise the distinct smell of algae that still hung in the air. The weight of the clouds was ready to break and eager to spill the snow-like frozen confetti which they too tightly held onto, and slowly, flakes began to fall. Large, light, and fluffy they glided down, floating like feathers landing effortlessly upon the cobbles. The atmosphere felt incredibly romantic and snuggled in their coats, neither said a word.

Blinking, Hannah peered up as the ice angels tumbled upon her lashes and nose as she childishly stuck her tongue out to catch them. Tom looked lovingly on, and she giggled joyfully welcoming a look she had long missed. They hadn't really shared 'time' like this and in that moment, neither existed in a world haunted by evil, and it was bliss.

It was mid to late afternoon as winters darkness crept in to close the day, but sparkling flakes illuminating, got in its way. The snow fell heavily and soon the town was covered, as it settled happily upon the bone-dry ground. Not a lamppost or ledge was left unglazed, coating the town, and slowing the pace.

Browsing the festive windows, tiny lights twinkled revealing the magic behind their panes. A carousel here, a candy cane filled tree there, and boxes of all shapes and sizes wrapped in red and green. Mr. and Mrs. Harrison had the 'The Man in the Red' Express Train, a trainset they bought out each Christmas. It shunted its way with the sound of clickety clack among the pies and cheeses and sitting at the helm of the tiny steamer was the man in red himself, Santa Claus.

The smell of jacket potatoes, roast chestnuts and sweet mulled wine filled the air, courtesy of Ben and Dale from the Bakers, who every Christmas erected specially monogramed gazebos that spilled out onto the streets. As ever, they dutifully, yet always quietly, provided an impeccable service. Standing in line for the roast chestnuts, it occurred to Hannah that Ben and Dale could be Naturals, the people blissfully unaware of the good versus evil forces that dwelt among them. Everyone though was born with the potential to receive 'The Gift' from The Great Star of The Cosmos. Among local unreceptive souls, without imaginary power, there was a rising fear about the age-old rumours surrounding the castle, causing severe unrest. Glossed over today, as the town congregated for the lighting ceremony by the town's Sea Stars, the relentless hardworking group of volunteers. Most of them, around a dozen in total, formed the choir that commenced the ceremony with each wearing a tabard with a star on the front and the back. They were busying themselves in preparation to switch on the Christmas tree lights. It was mostly Gifted Ones that joined the Sea Stars, particularly for this event, which was after all, a ceremony of light. As the choir gathered around the circumference of the tree, they broke into joyous song as the trees and the town became illuminated.

This was what Hannah had been waiting for and she was so excited to share it with Tom. It was jaw dropping for him; he had not seen anything like it before. Having been strictly raised under the control of the Watcher Crowcode, he was not used to such gaiety. Hannah felt this year she was viewing things differently, often the case of 'growing up' and for obvious reasons. Looking at Tom, today less anxious, she saw in his wide-eyed innocence her younger pre-Gifted self. A slight feeling of envy rushed over her followed by an innate sense of gratitude for what she now knew, and her pendant began to glow.

Preoccupied in her pleasure, she felt her attention awakened and drawn to the choir and Mr. and Mrs. Cox. Known for her bright sense of dress, underneath her tabard, she wore muted tones. She was certainly not 'singing her heart out' and instead, appeared full of anguish. Was she infected by The Watchers? Thoughts of seeing her in the Book of Spells came flooding back along with a fresh dose of nerves, prickling the perfect atmosphere. Hannah quickly switched to observe Mr. Cox. Usually a relaxed man, he stood tense. When it came to turning the page of the song sheet he did so in haste, rather angrily, almost ripping the sheet, quite clearly wanting the event to end. How different he seemed to the previous year, when he joyfully wore a pair of bright green earmuffs. Being bald headed, during winter he was known for wearing daft bobble hats, but this year only the snow decorated his head. Was he doubting his Gift as well? It certainly would link in with what her dad had said about him.

Mrs. Gives from school was of course in the choir. Her glasses were bouncing on her bosom as she sung to her hearts content, with her head tilted back. Her entire body was moving in the tabard, which due to her short stout physique was more than a snug fit. She was standing next to Mr. Harrison and side by side, they cut a funny couple. Standing tall, shadowing her, his tabard equally as tight, dangled below his butcher's apron. He sang with the same passion, in a loud, low, deep voice. His chest was thrust so far forward that his tabard was on the verge of ripping apart! Obviously, his thick woolly snood was keeping his vocal cords most warm.

Hannah chuckled to herself; she wished her dad was here. Together they would have shared the same sense of humour in it all. Thinking of her dad, she remembered the books she had noticed in his attic room, as with many of the locals, he also seemed to have changed.

Lost in thought, as she was prone to, it was remarkable how

amidst the noise she heard the gentle voice, "Hello dear." It was Ann, the Leader of the Belief Council, with her dog, peering down, leaning on her walker. "Looking forward to *really seeing* you soon dear." She spoke.

Being blind, she looked beyond Hannah, her dog held the same soft glaze, which was remarkable really for an animal in such a lively environment. He had mistletoe tied to his red collar and looked so sweet. "Oh yes, I am very much looking forward to it Ann."

The brief yet concise conversation held as much purpose as necessary.

You may be wondering, if The Watchers attended the lighting ceremony, and did they celebrate Christmas? Letting the darkness control their imaginations, they took pleasure in observing and spying on The Gifted Ones, so attending such events was paramount, usually hanging back, huddled together in the numerous alley ways, which was popular amongst younger Watchers.

Their Christmas contained light of a different nature, in the form of flames as they held vigils as an act of worship to The Great Gifted Nickolous. Tom was familiar with the sight of bonfires; Hannah though was yet to learn about the twisted way they celebrated.

Naturals celebrated the festivities in the same way as Gifted Ones, *but the bell of belief did not ring for them the way it rang for the Gifted.*

There were other apparent differences between The Watchers, The Gifted and Naturals.

The snow had deepened and as if by magic, footprints vanished as the fresh powder fell. The town was calling it a day, ready to hunker down and many of the festive stalls were hurriedly being packed away. Hand in hand, with smiles on their faces, Tom and Hannah, having enjoyed their time, strolled home as leisurely as they had arrived and Hannah happily continued the guided tour of her hometown for Tom. As they passed Mrs. Robinson's Fishmonger shop, Hannah peered down an alleyway to the right. It was a habit; many locals unknowingly did, checking out the nooks and crannies of the town. Lit more than usual by the snow, huddled deep in the alleyway was a thong of Watchers, amongst them Renee and Beth, they looked up and seeing Hannah began to at once taunt her.

"Hey Hannah, wait up." They said, running to the top of the alley. Seeing Tom who they looked up and down, continued to tease her.

"Hope there is enough 'panther power' to hold onto your pendant!" and they began flapping their arms in make believe flight, more flamboyant than before, showing off to impress Tom.

Putting his arm around Hannah protectively and gently, Tom whispered, "Come on, ignore them. Let's go home."

She knew he was right and just about to go, when behind the girls she saw something. Firstly, she thought she could see Amelia's silhouette, her hair was indistinguishable. At the same time, her pendant began pulsating and could feel its warmth. Then, arising in the distance amidst them, as a ghost, appeared parky. Life-sized, his eyes stared, intently ahead through the snow, she could see him clearly. Renee and Beth faded into the background and although she could feel Tom tugging her, she remained rooted. Parky paced slowly towards her and coming face to face, in his deep reassuring tones said,

"Eyes, mind and heart wide open. Believe." And himself faded away.

"Yeah, you're brainless to believe that stupid stuff." Renee blurted, oblivious to the majesty that had just walked amongst them. Hannah did not reply. Sometimes, silence speaks volumes. Tom wrapping his arm around her, ushered her away and turning his head over his shoulder gave the girls an icy cold look.

As before, it seems these challenges presented themselves purposely and, in this case, it made Hannah and Tom cross the road onto the other side of the street, where the chemist was. What was about to happen would give Hannah more intelligence in her fight against The Watchers.

Loyalty to The Great Gifted Nickolous was entrenched in every Watchers soul, making them subservient. This submissive behaviour was as powerful as the dark master himself, why else would an intelligent and diligent man like Don Surlin want to infect his customers?

As they approached his shop, it was not unusual towards the end of a day, to see customers wating in line. It was snowing quite heavily, and although she had to squint to focus, the eyes of Hannah's soul were wide open having listened clearly to Parky. Coming closer, she could see the chemists store sign changing shape, the snake was moving away from the bowl. Breaking away it stretched and slithered, developing white wings and the face of a crow. It then thrust itself up into the air before slowly coming down, floating above its sorry victim's head, emitting a grey energy.

It had to be The Great Gifted Nickolous and catching sight of Hannah, he hissed, shrinking back into the bowl. "Tom, look, look." she said under her breath, nudging him, gesturing towards the sign, not wanting to cause a distraction. By the time Tom had looked up, it had disappeared.

Arriving home, standing on the doorstep, Hannah turned to look at the castle. A few people were trudging towards its grounds. Trudging was perhaps the best way to describe their dazed stagger, it was like they were sleepwalking.

The castle would look stunning in the morning, she thought. *Beautiful on the outside, but certainly not on the inside. For in its dark depths, lay an even darker soul.*

Chapter Eleven

The Magic of Matriarchs

December 12th, Ashby-by-the-Sea.

The Timms' walled garden was flawless. Perfectly preserved, layer upon layer, the snow had settled, robing the statues, and carpeting the yard. Some of the potted plants had stretched and groaned and shaken off their frosted blankets, others remained cocooned under the ice. Inside, Christmas was beginning to feel somewhat staged. Everyone was going about the business of getting Christmas 'done' rather than letting the festivities naturally unfold, perhaps perpetuated by Tom staying through the holidays. As a rule, The Gifted Ones are not particularly good at 'faking' any kind of celebrations, let alone Christmas. So, although the family were trying hard to push on, Belinda, Hannah and Amelia were feeling robbed of their natural happiness and individually all struggling in their own ways. Tim had not addressed the obsessiveness Joy was showing towards Hannah's pendant, despite Belinda's nudges, spending much of his time in the attic room, detached from the family's goings on. Amelia was also devoting much time to her bedroom, but unsettled, at her desk one minute, pottering the next. The only thing that was constant was the tormented look she carried around. Belinda was edging towards wanting to control what she felt was becoming a 'disturbing' situation, even though she had a profound trust in The Star. What Hannah did not know was that her mother was about to be granted the Gift of self-control, enabling her to channel energy into Amelia, infusing her with the wonders of her Gift instead of trying to fix the situation herself. The Star always delivered at the right time.

The Watcher clouds had begun to arrogantly invade the Gifted areas. Lenticular in shape, the eye of the cloud had stretched resulting in better Watching capabilities. With the eyes came a smell like mould, leaving locals flummoxed at what they thought could only be a natural phenomenon, as well as sticking to Mrs. Gives' line of, a 'viral outbreak'.

The Watchers were getting darker and had successfully infected many of The Gifted Ones, leading them to the castle. So confident had they become, they were beginning to use tiny public address systems, like the ones they had used in the summer, carried in their Watchercrows claws. The squawks from the sirens only added to the Naturals confusion, as dazed captives were directed to their doom. On both sides, the clock was ticking, and Hannah felt the overriding need to race on in this part of her life, to fathom a way and find the truth of what was going on. Tom's courage had picked up pace and following Hannah's unnerving account with The Great Gifted Nickolous at the chemist, he had even volunteered to 'check out' Pocklington. She was getting closer now to understanding how she thought The Watchers were infecting The Gifted. The grey power force she saw emitted was much smaller than she had witnessed before. Was this the way they were extinguishing The Gifted Ones imaginary friends? It would be the magic of Mini once again that steered Hannah to finding the truth.

It was evening time, and the house was somewhat fragmented. Tom was in his bedroom calling his folks back home and Joy was charging in the attic room with Tim nearby, sat reading. Both girls had settled down on the couch by the twinkling lights of the Christmas tree with Belinda, to watch a film. Presents wrapped in red and green were beginning to magically appear under the tree along with a sprinkling of pine needles. The evening was of course all perfectly orchestrated in part by Belinda, working in unison with her mother, even down to persuading Tim to charge Joy earlier than usual. The movie they were watching was a classic, a firm family favourite watched time and time again. Belinda blurting out suddenly, said, "Oh, this is one of Mini's favourite films." A look to Hannah followed, triggering the panther pendant to glow, it was time for her to go; knowing full well this was fait accompli. With her sister's head burrowed into her mother's bosom and Belinda stroking her flaming red hair, Hannah's departure would go unnoticed. Without hesitation she wandered into the hall to Mini's portrait and the same hazy glow wrapped in a shaft of light flowed from it. In an instant, Hannah's imagination came to life, the light from her chest beamed as her pendant radiated. Hannah was delighted to see Mini, as Mini was to see her. "Oh, my beautiful darling Hannah, *in our darkest times our best works are revealed.* In the depths of uncertainty, the truth will be uncovered. You will find how The Gifted are being infected. You will find a way Hannah! And one more thing, do not give up on anyone, your dad, Tom, Joy or Amelia. Like your mother, you will be granted with all the tools you need."

"Mini, don't leave me." Hannah couldn't understand why she said that and felt a need to cling to her. As the cloudy haze began dispersing, she saw Mini's lips move saying, "Always together in heart."

It wasn't at all surprising that very night, Mini's prophecy was revealed in Hannah's dream. The Star spoke to The Gifted Ones not only through their dreams but anyway and anywhere. Nothing was impossible and the spirit of Parky lived on. It was his sacrifice in the Battle of Minds that elevated the word 'friendship' to another level. A legacy evident in Hannah's pendant which went on to glow throughout the night as she headed to bed.

With thoughts going through her mind, and much tossing and turning, Hannah lay awake most of the night. She peered out at Queen Nail a least half a dozen times, finding it hard to settle. It was not until the cuckoo clock struck midnight, and the familiar little people in their traditional German dress waltzed out of their alpine hut, that she finally drifted into a deep sleep and began to dream. Strangely, the dream started with the sound of the cuckoo clock ticking.

In her dream, the doors of the cuckoo clock flung open as tiny lizard style creatures with the face and beak of a crow began rapidly flying out. Ten, twenty at a time, pouring into the dining room, before escaping into the hall and up the stairs. Swarms of flying Watcherfish began to fill every room in the house, flapping their prehistoric looking wings in search of prey. Then, finding their target, who in her dream, happened to be poor Amelia, they flew around her head like bees around a honey pot, emitting a tiny grey force. The dream was quickly turning into a nightmare, Hannah broke out in a cold sweat. Within the grey power force striking Amelia's head, words began appearing. Doubt, fear, control, followed by other more personal negative words describing her personality such as perfectionist and overachiever. Hannah tossed and turned, trying to fathom out what The Watcherfish were doing. They were once again prancing upon The Gifted, putting their Gifts in jeopardy by filling their minds with doubt and highlighting their vulnerabilities. This was in addition to their existing power of having the capability to destroy aspects of a Gifted One's imagination. Hannah's dream followed the ghastly Watchers, with the ability to change size, polluting the minds of The Gifted by accessing them in a variety of ways, through windows, doors, any way they could. Perhaps the most distressing part of the dream was when she found herself walking amongst countless Gifted Ones towards the castle, surrounded by flying Watcherfish and Watchercrows of all sizes. This was part and parcel of The Watchers plan, having worked upon their prey, seducing them to succumb to the darkness, and in a trance, to the crypt of The Great Gifted Nickolous. From here, much of the dream became distorted. Flashes of the castle appeared with glimpses of a huge snake and a whoosh of white wings. Hannah found herself amongst other victims lined up against a stone wall, being subjugated to a terrifying beast and its unescapable grey power. She had witnessed this before at the Battle of Minds, the force which extinguishes a Gifted Ones imaginary friends, except this was more. Its potency indescribable; the terror incomprehensible.

Trying desperately hard to wake from the hellish nightmare, she finally felt herself coming around. Licking her lips, beads of sweat had gathered, and her hair was moist; the grey power still clearly visible in front of her. She could not quite work out if she was still dreaming, then suddenly, something flew directly into the grey line of power and within seconds the entire dream had ended and standing at the foot of the bed was Belinda.

"Darling, you were crying out, so I came to see if you were ok." She was whispering gently, careful not to awaken the house. Belinda wore proper pyjamas like Mini and her arms were wide open with a blanket of over shoulders. Sitting up Hannah rolled onto her knees and into her mother's embrace, the silkiness of her pyjamas felt comforting, reminding her of Mini again.

"Oh, Hannah, it must have been a nightmare, you're all sticky" running her fingers through her tangled hair. "Something flew into The Watchers power Mum; I am so confused."

"It's all coming together now, Hannah. Remember darling, you're not alone. Much is asked of favoured ones, but no more than can be handled. My brave girl, look down." She was of course referring to Parky on her pendant, Hannah could see it was still glowing. She was right, his spirit was with her always.

"Come, tell me about your dream and together, we can make sense of it. Shall we see if Mini wants to join us?" It was a leading question, typical of her mother already knowing the answer. Hannah had the same feeling at the beginning of summer, that she was being drawn into the unknown, and in a way once again, it was rather exciting. In that moment, she felt an immense sense of gratitude for her mother and grandmother; matriarchs of the family and incredibly strong women.

So having followed her mother down the stairs, soon enough their bright lights shone, and their imaginations came to life and Mini appeared. Having the urge to share many things Hannah sensed her recent dream really was all they wanted to hear about. Ears, mind, and heart always open, both matriarchs listened attentively. It was cold, and sitting on the stairs, looking up to the portrait, Belinda wrapped her blanket around Hannah's shoulders as Mini began to talk.

"Hannah, I need to tell you about Victor." His name alone made her shudder and immediately she wondered if Mini was about to reveal his whereabouts, having already sensed Belinda knew something about him. "I told you how it saddened me, Victor defecting to The Watchers. His parents were our Godparents, we were family and being the same age and growing up together, we shared so much. It proves that we need to stay alert to the spirit of The Great Gifted Nickolous, intervening into the gulf of despondency with our loved ones." Hannah and Belinda immediately both thought of Amelia and Tom. "The good news is that after the Battle of Minds, The Great Star overcame Victor's darkness. Taking everything into account, even the smallest of things, such as his eyes softening every time he saw Tom, all proved he was still capable of loving. In Tom, he saw his younger self. The hurt I supposedly caused with his unrequited love for me, broke his heart. Nothing goes unnoticed by The Star. However, The Great Gifted Nickolous punished him for not seizing Parky in The Battle of Minds and transformed him permanently into a Watchercrow. The Great Star created a new beginning for him, in Ashby-by-the-Sea. Like Doodle, his penance is to live among the Watchers and to protect you, Hannah. He lives in the trees that line Castle Walk, the link between Ashby and Pocklington."

'Was he part of the frenzy of mad cawing crows she encountered when she visited Pocklington?' She thought. Interceding her thought pattern, Mini stressed, "You will know him by the leather necklace he still wears with a pendant of a crow. He will help us." It was all dawning upon her. Maybe it was Victor blocking The Watchers power in her dream? Was he the crow that she had seen in the Book of Spells trying to divert Tom's unicorn? She wondered randomly, if Tom would have recognised his necklace, and if Victor eyes would have softened, if not edged in fear? Probably not. Belinda could see it all racing around in her mind and wrapping things up, bid her mother farewell. "Goodnight." She said to Mini blowing her a kiss. "I think that's quite enough for one night. We will take it all to the Belief Council." Mini winked, drifting away, and Belinda and Hannah headed back to their beds.

Amelia banged her fists upon her pillow. She had woken about the time Belinda had gone into Hannah's room. She crept around to her room and listened to their plan of talking with Mini. She then hung back until they had gone downstairs and crept round to the top of the stairs, crouching there, she listened to everything Belinda and Mini had said.

She felt excluded just as all those years ago Victor must have. Worst of all she felt sick with jealously, which she hated. Just then, the most horrible thoughts began to enter her head on ways she might feel better. The dark power was prancing on poor Amelia.

The battle would begin, and The Gifted Ones would need their imaginary friends, now more than ever.

Chapter Twelve

Jigsaw Cottage

It was now December 18th. The Belief Council were due to meet. The meeting was crucial for many reasons, particularly with The Spectacle Council having such a strong foothold in Ashby-by-the-Sea. "Dress smart." Belinda said jokingly to Hannah, before quickly adding, "Only joking darling, better to be smarter on the inside than the out." Hannah, nevertheless, wore a white shirt with a pale pink cardigan, trimmed in red satin; it was quite festive. Her pendant had not stopped glowing.

Passing by Amelia's room, she poked her head around the door, she was at her desk gazing out of the window. 'Did her 'virus of the mind' all those weeks ago accumulate in her deciding to place the desk with a direct view of the castle? A direct view of the final resting place for The Great Gifted Nickolous, father of all Watchers?

"See you later." Hannah said, trying to distract her from her forlorn gaze. Looking around, flicking her hair, firstly she checked Hannah up and down, seeing what she was wearing, before concluding her sultry stare, as usual, at her pendant. "Yeah, don't rub it in."

"Amelia, you must trust me." Authoritatively, she stepped into her room and going over to her, a tear came to Amelia's eye. Without further ado, Amelia stood up from her chair and they hugged. She almost fell into her arms, if anything, almost clinging onto Hannah.

Seeing Amelia like this saddened her and made her feel angry. The Watchers were closing in on her very own family. Pulling away, both held on to each other's arms and looking directly into her eyes, Hannah said, "I got this."

Waiting at the bottom of the stairs were Tom and Belinda.

"Good luck! Hope it goes ok." Tom said cheerily, before tenderly kissing the top of her head. "I'll see what your dad is up to; hopefully we can spend some time together." She appreciated Tom's suggestion. She had told him she had missed chatting with her dad; he seemed so distant.

"It's time to believe darling." Belinda said, placing Hannah's peacoat over her shoulders. And with those words they crunched their way through the snow to Jigsaw Cottage.

Thinking like her father, and planning like her mother, she had already made a mental note of what she would like to discuss at the meeting. The list went as follows:

1. Pocklington's Spectacle Council in the Gillaweep Brook.

2. The Great Gifted Nickolous (The GGN)- the winged snake with the face and beak of a crow. It made her wince as she recalled him.
3. Mr. Surlin and The GGN appearance at the Chemist.
4. Her dream of how The Watchers were targeting The Gifted.
5. Victor.

Hannah would learn that meetings at The Belief Council, never take on such a controlled agenda, it was more a case of lettings things evolve. "Well, here we are." Belinda said, lightly knocking Ann's door.

Her mother, as ever, did look smart and 'well put together.' Today's ensemble consisted of a tweed skirt suit with a feather trim collar and a shirt like Hannah. Her Belief necklace was on full show. Waiting for the door to be opened, Hannah turned round to look down Market Street. Jigsaw Cottage really did hold the finest views of the town and one could see everything.

Maria, one of The Belief Council members, opened the door. Smiling at them both, it wasn't long before Walter, Ann's dog, came snuffling over. He had the same red collar on, with a new sprig of mistletoe. The room, much like the Timm's home, was filled with festive aromas. Pine and a notable smell of frankincense filled the air. Sitting in the corner of the room, in a big chair covered in a lemon-coloured checked fabric, was Ann. Her soft mysterious face smiled. "Welcome my dears," she said gently. "Let us join the others in the conservatory."

Slowly, they followed her through. In the far distance Hannah could hear the chitter chatter of voices along with the sounds of flowing water and wind rustling through trees and over grasslands, the sounds of nature. As she entered the conservatory, all its dimensions changed.

It was just as her mother had said, idyllic surroundings in a perpetual light. Hannah was astounded at the beauty inside and didn't know where to look first. It was how she imagined it to be, the Garden of Eden. Even though she was standing on the ground, it had an ethereal effect, she was somewhat overwhelmed. Belinda tenderly put her arm around her. "Beautiful, isn't it?"

"It is not just the beauty I can see, but the beauty I can feel." She replied profoundly, captivated by the unspoilt natural beauty surrounding her. In the distance, running down one of the rolling hills Hannah thought she could see Mini with Doodle. Her heart leapt, but wondered how she could see Doodle, knowing she had passed. Then, over the crest of the same hill and walking at a steady pace were Nancy and William, her Great Grandparents. Mini had told her once she wished she had known if her parents were Gifted, maybe seeing them here they were.

Higher up in the space a huge rainbow began to form, its colours more vibrant than Hannah could ever imagine, and sliding down were her imaginary friends from the summer, Nancy the Lamp, followed by the young Mini from the painting.

"Can you see them all darling?" Belinda whispered gently in her ear. "Family and friends, including our imaginary friends, all exist here as well as in our subconscious, for many reasons. Think of them as guardian angels, to warn and protect us. You may have already seen them from time to time." Indeed, she had. Nancy the lamp in Pocklington, and maybe even young Mini from the painting in Joy.

It was all racing around in her head, when Mr. and Mrs. Cox came by, giving her a tight smiled nod, before being ushered on by Mrs. Gives. "Over to the lake, everybody!" Ann was rounding everyone up to start the ceremony and meeting. There were twelve of them in total. The lake seemed to stretch into a never-ending horizon behind her, as she stood in front of the eleven.

"It's Time to Believe!" Ann announced quietly yet joyously, opening the meeting, everyone clapped and cheered, Mr. Harrison more so. The formal proceedings had begun, and Hannah was presented with the necklace of Belief. As Ann placed it around her neck, Mrs. Gives helped fasten it. The word 'Believe', hung from the necklace and sat directly above the panther pendant.

It was then that in the distance, appeared Parky. Smiling warmly with loving eyes, his wings were fully extended, mightier, and whiter than ever before. There was more cheering and clapping, as his presence signified that Hannah was a favoured Gifted One. Next came the introspection part of the meeting. Belinda had explained to Hannah that this could be described as a mental health check.

Each member took turns to peer into the lake, their reflections highlighted areas of personal development to work upon, an examination of conscious. They then stood face to face with Ann who, having been Gifted with the liberty of seeing the state of their souls, brought everything together, placing it into the bigger picture.

Their family members were also brought to Ann's attention as nothing was missed under the guidance of The Great Star. All of this was explained to Hannah by Mrs. Gives as she stood watching by the lake. Following this the group convened and council matters were addressed. Almost always, these issues were corrected following the introspection process, and items naturally concluded. Having listened carefully to Hannah and Belinda, Ann confirmed that both Tom and Amelia's souls were sadly drifting towards the darkness of The Watchers. Their devious methods were feeding doubt into Amelia.

Hannah felt a flash of jealousy, she had recognised it in her reflection. Now, having had it confirmed by Ann, she understood the need to address the emotion as it would not be conducive to the long-term plan.

"Belinda, following your increased strength in self-control, I think you will now find it easier to accept that Tim is most unsettled. It is not for me to reveal this to you completely. All I can tell you is..." Then, turning to Hannah, she concluded what Belinda needed to know and said, "In the dark he will decide." It sounded like a riddle. Ann in many ways reminded her of Mini.

Belinda took it calmly, even though she was swaying in sadness, for she loved Tim but was not surprised, she had noticed his 'absence' for a while.

Knowing Joy, the AI was treated with respect in the Timms family, Ann went onto to say that irrespective of her not having a soul, it was important that she was treated responsibly. She then addressed the rest of the members before talking again with Hannah and Belinda,

"The Watchers are utilising technology inappropriately, having already introduced Cawcams."

Which was the enhanced AI Watcher, able to record everything in ultra-high definition with their camera eyes.

Unexpectedly entering the space, seemingly from nowhere appeared a Watchercrow. Startled she nudged her mother, but before she responded she was side-tracked by the others muttering and heard someone say, "Oh, it's Victor." Looking up, Hannah somehow did recognise him. She was astounded that Victor was now her 'protector.'

He flew down to Ann's ear and spoke to her. "Dear members, Victor has news." He reported to Ann that Joy had been spying on the Gifted and was infected by The Watchers. Thankfully, he had managed to intercede the situation and Joy had only reported information to him, thinking he was a Watchercrow.

Hannah's face fell blank and staring into space, she herself began to piece it all together. When she'd seen Joy in The Book of Spells, it was Victor she was relaying all the information to and that was why she couldn't see who it was.

"Thank you, Victor." Ann said bidding him farewell, and he flew back to Castle Walk.

Moving on, next Ann made sure that Hannah was privy to Mrs. Cox's introspection as her reflection revealed a foray of anxiety. She had been worrying excessively about her husband becoming infected by The Watchers. In fact, the growing fiasco between The Watchers and The Gifted Ones had made her anxious for some time. She had been overthinking and trying to fight everyone's battles, including Bob the postman. She was certain that The Watchers were preying on him as well. Bravely, out of her own inquisitiveness, she had ventured around Pocklington. Seeing Joy there she had ruthlessly purged what information she could from her, misusing and abusing the technology of an AI. Worst of all she was acting on her own intuition, choosing to follow her own instinct, rather than listening to The Great Star, crushing the openness of her Gift to trust with a full heart and mind.

Following Mrs. Cox, Ann concluded the meeting. Slowly, clearly, and concisely she said, "The Watchers have a desire not only to eliminate our bountiful Gift, but also to do everything to obstruct our belief. We must always remember that The Great Gifted Nickolous believes that by stealing power from others will increase his own. So, my friends, what is the way forward? The Watchers main objective is to destroy their greatest threat, Parky the panther, whose spirit lives on. They will not cease their chase until they have seized Hannah's panther pendent. Their quest is futile, we need to remain impartial. We need to seek a reconciliation, to try to come together. We should try our best not to translate their actions as complicity with evil. Hannah will lead and report."

There were a few eyebrows raised then quickly dropped as the truth resounded, then everyone clapped and were joyful in renewed in hope.

"THANK you," said Hannah. Ann was back in her big bright armchair with Walter loyally by her side. "I have every ounce of faith in you my dear," she replied. "And, as your grandmother often reminds you, 'Always together in heart.'"

And her panther pendent continued to glow.

Chapter Thirteen

Saving Souls

A feeling of anticipation, not only for Christmas, had paved the way for renewed hope within the Timms household, easing tensions surrounding Amelia and Tim. Tom, it seemed, had gained strength, supporting Hannah. Their relationship had strengthened, having confided deeply in one another. In a few days it was set to be a white Christmas and having grown a beard, Tim now needed a red suit to complete the festive look. However, it was not in the traditional seasonal spirit that he had decided to grow it. He had become so consumed in his own thoughts that he had begun to neglect himself. Belinda patiently and lovingly supported him whenever he would allow her to.

During this unsettled time, Queen Nail, eager to see living waters run clean in the battle of The Watchers and The Gifted Ones, appeared floating above the pond in the garden. Hannah intuitively felt Queen Nail calling her. With her powerful energy rising and the pendent glowing, she grabbed her coat and headed outside as the beam of light burst forth from her chest. Seeing her go, like Mini, Belinda winked, knowing once again her daughter's time had come. Hannah's imaginary Gift combined with the spiritual connection she shared with Queen Nail, perfected their synergy. Majestically she floated above the pond. It was daytime and against the back-drop of the walled garden she exuded the presence of an ice Queen. The luxurious velvet of her blue tunic appeared sumptuous against the white snow and the colours of her tail sparkled. Her silver hair stiffened, as she bore the weight of the crown of stars, which today, were shimmering sky high. She looked more glorious than ever, a Queen ready for battle and to add to her glory appeared The Great Star of the Cosmos, who's rays, lucid in the daylight, seemed to touch the garden wall melting the snow around them.

Slinking stealthily down one of the particularly thick rays, with his wings hung limp, one paw at a time, was no other than Parky the Panther. He leapt the short space from the ray onto the garden wall, sinking into the snow before slightly shaking himself.

"It is time to see the full picture, Hannah." He said in his deep voice, extending a paw to her.

Queen Nail gently smiling, outreached her palms towards Hannah in the direction of Parky, gesturing her towards him. Raising a hand towards his paw and no sooner had they touched, that Hannah in one fell swoop, was raised up, toppling onto his back. She flung her arms around his neck and nestled her face into his fur, it was heavenly. Turning his head, she could see the profile of a warm smile. It was just like old times, and he reminded her of her Gifted obligations.

"Hold tight, *only if you believe can you make the impossible possible.*"

The long rays of The Great Star retracted and in one almighty leap, Parky was airborne and together they soared as they had before and neither spoke a word. Within seconds, looking down upon Ashby-by-the-Sea it resembled a matchbox town blanketed in snow.

Ahead of them, twinkling in the distance, was a dazzling arch. It was the *'Bridge of Stars'*. She sensed she had dreamt what she was experiencing and drawing closer, it became clear. The stars were all different, some broken, some chipped, some shorter or longer and some, at times, shone brighter than others with different rays. *They all shone in different ways, but together they made a dazzling arch, a beautiful bridge.*

Over the bridge they began to descend and from afar things became familiar, but a galactic haze framed everything they saw. Hannah had experienced it at Mini's the day she received the Book of Spells from Doodle.

As they gently landed, she knew they were on the higher ground where the caves existed, a little way behind their home. This was the first place Parky wanted her to see.

Even through the haze, Hannah could smell the musty earth oozing from the wide-open dark mouths of the small natural caves, which were more like grottos. Parky could see her wondering why he had bought her here. "The Unsaid live here Hannah, Naturals who have decided to live a solitary lifestyle whilst seeking a change of heart in their belief. Some Unsaid go on to realise their Gift but decide to remain here, living in seclusion. Deep voids for soul searching."

As Parky spoke, standing behind her, she could feel his breath on her neck, and turning around they stared into each other's eyes but neither said a word. There was strange, otherworldly sensation that surrounded the caves.

The next place they arrived at was not far away, around Pocklington. The small, gently flowing Flushing Waterfalls, surrounded by mossy plants. Side by side, they stood at the top looking over them. "These are like the Flushing Meadows, Hannah. The Watcherfish, seeking redemption, fly and perform a series of jumps here, in the hope of attracting The Great Stars attention."

As he spoke, she recalled the cleansing process, remembering it being risky and highly forbidden, The Watchers did not take kindly to betrayal, as Mini had previously told her.

On their next stop, they passed by the castle, landing by the ruins of an old amphitheatre. Known around the town as 'The Arena.' Now unused and overlooked, in its day, the large circular open-air venue with its raised seating would have provided a source of entertainment. "Over the centuries, this historic site has been used by The Mindful Watchers for vigils to venerate The Great Gifted Nickolous" Parky told her. Something Hannah would be privy to in only a few days' time.

Before they headed back over The Bridge of Stars, they flew over the 'Star of the Sea' church with its huge limestone tower. As they glided over, Hannah had an instinctive feeling telling her this was a safe place.

Back over The Bridge of Stars, in no time at all, they landed safely in the Timm's walled garden, where Queen Nail who navigates on all levels, not just in water, was waiting patiently. Ready to guide her, organise a supper and seek reconciliation with The Watchers.

"I don't understand it all." she said to Parky whist dismounting him. "You will, when the time is right," he replied. "I am with you always." And looking at the pendant, said, "Just keep believing." He leapt onto the wall and into the creamy sky, disappearing into the distance.

"Come dear," Queen Nail said, hovering over the iced pond, "We have work to do." And she extended her hand, inviting her to take it. As her powerful, imaginative energy rose, Hannah felt herself being raised up and the beam of light burst forth from her chest, transforming her into a mermaid. Together, they both dropped seamlessly, cutting through the ice, into the underworld of The Watchers.

Once in the water, Hannah became acquainted with her ability to breathe, hear, and talk and for a moment, she marvelled at her mermaid tail, every shade of white imaginable. She felt in awe of her Gifted power as she observed the fish swimming and plants swaying in the current, the beauty of the wet world, even though it was rather dark and immersed under a blanket of ice. Queen Nail swam ahead, turning round momentarily, checking her charge. Stopping, she flipped around to talk with Hannah. "We will be shrouded once again in the 'Armour of Light.' Only when we reach the council chamber and encounter Mr. Surlin, the protective barrier will be released. Remember, The Watchers will be drawn to your power and your mindful energy. You must never forget their ability to destroy aspects of your imagination. Always be on your guard. Eventually, they will be the ones caught off guard, not us."

The crown of stars provided protection immediately and in safety they continued their journey.

Watcherfish appeared, the water turned into a muddy colour as the area became narrower and more restricted. Soon enough, they came across a huge shoal of Watchers waiting to pass into another part of the brook, under the arch, where the 'Spectacle Council' was held.

The meeting had already commenced and as they passed by the rock, suspended by old rotten rope, denoting that they were now in the chamber, motions were being passed, under the item of 'Battle Plan.'

At the front was Mr. Surlin, along with the eleven other council members, all wearing the winged snake pendant. They formed two lines of five with the eleventh member next to Mr. Surlin.

Many other Watcherfish suddenly joined the chamber, and the waters became turbulent, as if a feeding frenzy were taking place, there was much anticipation and excitement as the leader was about to rally the troops.

"My children. These waters run wild with the spirit of The Great Gifted Nickolous and I assure you, that one day soon, these waters will rise and shower The Gifted, washing their power away." Hannah was transfixed by the bubbles spilling out of his fish mouth as he spoke. She began to realise that maybe her dream of being transported on the Gillaweep brook in a wooden boat was a prophecy, or insight, fulfilling the myth that a boat transported the casket of The Great Gifted Nickolous along these waterways. Mr. Surlin went on to rouse the school, "We fly as a bird with the fluidity of a fish."

Every time he finished a sentence, the frenzy would fire up again and the waters became choppy. Hannah was wondering when she should approach him and if it was too much of a risk losing the 'Armour of Light.'

"I will guide you dear." Queen Nail said, reading her mind.

"First we flame and honour him at The Arena tomorrow!" the leader said defiantly. His closing statement was met with rapturous flapping from Watcherfish. He was referring to the vigil, and in that moment, maybe knowing she would have need to attend it, Hannah's bravery reached a new level. Receptive to her, Queen Nail nodded and the 'Armour of Light' was dropped.

'Still rivers may run deep, whilst wild waters wonder,'

Seeing a favoured Gifted One gracing their presence made all The Watchers look on in amazement. The glow from her pendant lit up the entire Council chamber. The snake in Mr. Surlin's eyes simultaneously slithered from side to side uncontrollably as he was caught off guard. "Returning to play in the puddles, are we?" he said sarcastically swimming closely up to her. "Or are we venturing into the big brook now?" Laughing, even the bubbles from his mouth seemed corrupt, odd in shape, each breath poisonous, she thought.

"Mr. Surlin, The Gifted Ones would like to meet with The Watchers. How about supper at the castle?" Hannah had not planned what to say and found the words tumbled out in a polite, yet assertive fashion. Some of the schools of fish were gathering slowly around her, with eyes on her pendant. Queen Nail wafted closely behind. "The castle? Why of course!" he jested, not taking her invitation at all seriously. Clearly astounded and somewhat charmed, he laughed again, and more crooked bubbles flowed from the cracks of his fish mouth.

"Oh, we wouldn't miss it for the *WORLD Hannah!*" he replied sarcastically. Snapping out his laugh, he swam up close making eye contact. His drastic movement made her flip backwards and her tail caused a slight wake in the water thrusting some of Watcherfish back.

Gaining composure, she confidently confirmed their supper date. "So, Mr. Surlin, 11pm, the day after Christmas."

"Oh, what a banquet it will be!" he replied, mocking her, before seriously instructing her, "Make sure you are *ALL* there." Then he swam back to the eleven and engaged in what looked like a deep discussion.

The Armour of Light surrounded them both as they swam swiftly back to the pond in the Timm's garden. Hannah was propelled out of the ice and peering back over the pond, she could see Queen

Nail below. "We have a date, Hannah. Ann will be pleased. '*The Star always Shines upon those that Shine*' and today, my dear, you were radiant." Hannah watched her slowly disappearing, along with the glow from her crown of stars, as she drifted down deep into the pond.

Walking back into the house, the sweet smell of cinnamon met the warmth of a freshly lit fire. Hannah was so happy to see everyone sitting at the kitchen table, even if it was a mixed reception.

Tom and Belinda both stood up immediately and within seconds Belinda had flung her arms, fussing around her. Tim sat with his head hung low but managed a smile as he tilted his head. His beard was now full and thick, and he sat nervously ruffling his red hair. Amelia's eyes reflected the relief of Hannah's home coming, but neither she nor Tim moved.

A huge responsibility hung over Hannah, not only to meet her family's needs, but that of The Gifted. As the crown of stars weighed heavy upon Queen Nail, so too did her mission to end the futile feud.

Normally this close to Christmas, carol singers in bonnets and top hats with red trimmed velvet capes, would be adorning the doorsteps in song. With the town in turmoil and the Watcher clouds prevalent, Christmas this year would not be normal. Walking upstairs to bed, Mini winked at her from the portrait. Just like Parky, she was always with her. Hannah had her grandmother's steely determination. Everything was falling into place, starting tomorrow with The Arena.

Chapter Fourteen

Part One – Panther at the Opera
Part Two – Believe on Christmas Eve

Panther at the Opera

Beneath the blanket of snow which nestled nicely upon the town of Ashby-by-the-Sea, the familiar smell of mould and algae lurked. Bursts of the odours kept the locals bewildered and The Gifted-on guard.

Following her recent encounter with Mr. Surlin, Hannah remained hopeful, sharing the events of the meeting with her family. By doing so, she thought it held them together, in a joint mission and diverted any neglective feelings Amelia may be harbouring. This was very much a joint Gifted operation, of which at this stage, she was at the helm. Today, she would venture to The Arena, in the hope that she may further understand why The Watchers had lost faith and belief in the Gift they had been so graciously granted. She hadn't conceived any of it, but plans unfurled as the unfathomable experiences did. With Queen Nail accompanying her, she would be guarded in the Armour of Light and able to watch the vigil without The Watchers aware of her presence. It was all part of The Star's plan and Hannah was receptive. She was simply exploring and cultivating, because ultimately The Watchers which could be redeemed, was out of her hands.

The vigil was held at The Arena from dusk until dawn which gave Hannah the opportunity of spending the day with her family although feeling festive was proving difficult. As ever, Belinda made every effort to organise and generally keep everyone as happy as she could, without being controlling.

As Hannah headed to meet Queen Nail in the garden, she felt brave and on track with fulfilling her mission. The personal desire for home and relationships to return to normal kept her driven, believing that the conflict with The Watchers could be resolved once and for all. This courageous confidence was crucial for what she was about to witness at The Arena.

Meeting at the pond, Queen Nail explained that today she would use her Gift in a new way. Hannah was dressed in her normal attire of jeans, hoody, and her peacoat, with the addition of a white bobble hat. Together hand in hand, they mystically manoeuvred their way to The Arena. Coated in a sprinkling of powdery snow, the Arena's architectural remains appeared stunning, but not one single Watcher was to be seen. "We will have to enter their imaginary shield to spectate." Queen Nail gently whispered to her. "This is the reason Parky brought you here to prepare your mind. Together, under the Armour of Light, we shall use our powers to transport us there."

Nothing is impossible for those who believe, so with her light shining bright and pendant glowing she found herself at the opening of what appeared to be an ancient roman amphitheatre. Standing at the entrance was a guard, dressed in a black cape. He or she seemed to have the body of a human, with the face and wings of crow and a sword could be seen coming out of the back of its body, piercing through a cape that fitted its grotesque frame. "I wonder what the sword is for?" Hannah asked Queen Nail. "To slash the belief of being Gifted." she replied. Wincing, she did not want to imagine how or why such a thing existed and worked.

They ventured into the large circular open-air venue. Its raised seating rose steeply and at the top panning the perimeter were flamed torches.

In the middle of the Arena, well distanced apart, could be seen a few things. Firstly, a huge stage with steps leading up to an almighty sized rectangular shaped glass tank, filled to the brim with water. Then secondly, what seemed to look like the foundations of a bonfire. There was much jeering and jollity as Watchers of all ages were walking up to the unlit firepit and tossing what looked like personal possessions onto it. Hannah recalled Tom sharing details of vigils he had attended from his Watcher days. Rocking horses, swings, dolls, pictures, all once meaningful possessions and probably valued imaginary friends, were tossed, like scraps to a dog, in preparation to go up in flames. Some Watchers, once their offerings had been presented, transformed into crows, flying back to their seats. They all abided by The Watcher dress code of black. Women, according to their age, in long or short gypsy skirts and men in heavy jeans, thick sturdy belts and open necked shirts. All their garments featured festive accents. The men for instance, had smart snakeskin boots or jackets, whilst over the women's blouses, their shawls or jackets featured feathers or snakeskin adornments. Some of the younger Watchers had feathers in their wild untamed hair and wore heavy dark makeup, making their pale skin appear translucent in the dusk light. All jewellery worn denoted either crows or snakes and most elders wore such necklaces or multiple bracelets.

Standing on the steps of the stage was a rather plump lady wearing a black cape, donned in multiple layers of feathers and a very tall hat in the shape of a twisted cone made of snakeskin. She seemed to be the master of ceremonies and began singing in a rather shrill, supreme voice, reminiscent of an opera singer. Her song recounted the words of Mr. Surlin, "*We fly as a bird with the fluidity of a fish. Oh, The Great Gifted Nickolous, Come.*" The crowd clapped and repeatedly began chanting again and again, "*Slash and Burn Belief! Slash and Burn Belief! Slash and Burn Belief.*"

Watchers were burning relics of objects that once ignited their imaginations from when they were Gifted and believed. Strangely, in this absurd gathering, they were also exchanging presents with another, approved by the Watchers Crowcode. Mr. Surlin threw his offering on the bonfire and sitting close by, she could see Renee and Beth giggling, as they exchanged gifts.

Food vendors wearing T-shirts emblazoned with the motif '*Flame On*', were located on the ground level of the Arena. Selling mostly *'fishy eyes'* better known as cockles and mussels or *'speckled balls'*, which were boiled eggs with pepper and mayonnaise. They were served in small glass jars with long spiral shaped spoons, with the head of a fish. Regular drinks were available with the most popular being *'BrookBale'*, a beer which incorporated precious water from the Gillaweep brook.

With a rapturous roar from the crowd, Mr. Surlin, Leader of The Spectacle Council, lit the bonfire and smoke twirled and twined its way into the sky before flames took flight.

Hannah felt afraid and looked at Queen Nail in a maternal way, as a young daughter would her mother. Her confidence had waned, and she was finding the entire event intimidating. She was privy to the authentic world of The Watchers, who in this setting seemed self-assured, making her doubt her plans of meeting them, knowing they had their own sordid battle ideas. Drawing in the Armour of Light, Queen Nail mindfully pulled Hannah in closer. The gesture along with the warmth from her pendant reassured her.

She would need it for what was to occur next.

As the fire ferociously fed upon The Watchers disbelief, the most grotesque Watcher specimen appeared. It was of course The Great Gifted Nickolous, monster of monsters. Within the rectangular glass tank, accessed from the dark depths of the castle crypt, emerged a giant slithering snake, whose white wings had transformed into fins as it propelled its black body in a swirling dervish. With the face and beak of a crow, memories of her encounter at the castle flooded back. The snake went to the side of the tank, he knew she could see, coldly staring in her direction. It made her blood run cold. His stare was hypnotizing and with it a feeling of being pulled down into the depths of the earth. Just then, at the top of the Arena, something was flying around its perimeter. It instantly broke the snakes spell and within seconds Hannah came to recognise it as Parky the Panther. Flying around in a blaze of glory, his huge, majestic wings whooshed, creating a powerful wind unlike any other.

Most Watchers were startled but then something remarkable happened. Some of them, stood up from their seats, drawn to Parky's incredible energy, the ultimate prize. Others remained seated, focusing on ways they could expel their powerful force upon him, but not for long, as their stone seats became as hot as the fires of hell, making it impossible for them to sit down. Parky had intervened his way, the only way, in the hope of raising their spirits.

The gigantic serpent was infuriated, propelling himself out of the water, with his destructible power force, in the direction of Parky. Relentlessly up and down, he jabbed into the darkness as Parky whipped around like the wind. Eventually, when each Watcher had stood up, Parky vanished and the Serpent dropped into the tank, back into the depths of the crypt.

Part Two: Believe on Christmas Eve

Hannah, out of fear, was worried that the disturbance at the Arena would jeopardise her meeting with The Watchers, fuelling their anger. Home, back in the Timm's garden, Queen Nail confirmed, "If it is in the plan of The Great Star Hannah, nothing will get in the way. Keep trusting and believing." And she froze, returned to the silence of a statue, back on the steps.

She was reminded yet again of being surrounded by women of admirable strength and back in the house, seeing Mini wink at her, filled her with pride as she tiptoed up to bed. So many layers of emotions existed, not only from the night's events at the Arena. Confusion over her dad, sentimental concern for her mum, and worry over Tom, but also the profound sadness and frustration for Amelia, tormented by the perverse beast she had just witnessed. It was weighing heavy.

The next morning would be a Christmas Eve the family would never forget. Hannah put her restless night's sleep down to unsettledness, as well as the obvious unprecedented events in her life. What she didn't yet know, was that her disturbed feeling went beyond mental concern, because in the night, evil had crept into her room. Amelia had been tipped over the edge. It was around the time Parky had aroused the interest of The Watchers in the Arena and the darkness had taken control, although her family, for a while, would be unaware of her treacherous deed.

It was the news that Tim was nowhere to be seen in the house, which took precedence that snowy Christmas Eve morning. "Let me take a walk out and look." Tom kindly suggested. Whilst Hannah had been otherwise occupied, he had got to know the local area quite well. Belinda was unusually calm, clearing the breakfast plates, whilst Joy washed the dishes. It certainly helped Hannah's anxiety about her father, but tripled Amelia's helplessness, as she was blaming herself for their father's disappearance.

"I am sure your father will be back soon, after all its Christmas Eve." Belinda confidently reassured the girls; she knew something was amiss but in the great scheme of things Tim's behaviour had culminated to something she fully accepted was out of her control. Amelia, guiltily, kept her head down.

"You don't think he's been taken by The Watchers, do you?" Hannah whispered to Tom in the hall, whilst he put on his leather jacket. "Now, you are letting your imagination run away with you!" He playfully joked whilst cuddling her trying to lighten the situation. Pulling away, he looked down to her pendant. "Hey where's your Parky necklace?" Hannah looked down; she was still in her pyjamas. Her Belief necklace was there but the panther pendant had gone.

This is what had happened. Amelia had dreamt about taking possession of Hannah's pendant, consuming her in the night, and she had woken with a plan to steal it. She had misused her imaginative Gift, using her power to bring Joy to life and manipulating the snake bracelets which graced her Amazonian body, to slither into Hannah's room, coil around her chain and snap it from her. When the dirty deed was done, she had suddenly heard someone in the hall. It was Tim, stuffing a large backpack with a couple of blankets. He had then headed briefly to the kitchen. Consumed in guilt, she dropped the pendant still on the necklace into the backpack, without a thought of where her father was heading and creeped back into bed.

"Mum!" Hannah yelled from the hall, having let Tom out in search for Tim. "Both my Parky pendant *and* Dad have gone!" Running into the kitchen, in disbelief, Hannah pulled at her pyjama top revealing the absence of the pendant to her mother. Amelia, sitting at the table, glanced up sideways flicking her hair in a surly fashion. Belinda remained resolute. In time, there would be a perfectly adequate reason explaining the departure of two of the most precious things in her life. "Come on girls." She said opening her arms wide beckoning them both in. Each fell into her bosom, and began to cry for quite different reasons, yet in solidarity for the same cause, for the bitter battle between The Watchers and The Gifted Ones to end.

The three women knew there must be a reason behind Tim's departure and the missing pendant. Hannah looked at Amelia across her mother's bosom, she knew Amelia had something to do with it all yet was not in the slightest angry with her.

"Let us make cookies and wait for Tom to get back! We must continue to believe that everything will work out in the end." Amidst it all Belinda kept the show on the road and wearing her 'Christmas Eve' sweater, both girls, mother and Joy set about baking cookies and drinking hot chocolate.

For Tim, Christmas Eve couldn't have been more different. In the early hours, he had arrived where he needed to be, with the Unsaids, at the caves. He knew that no matter how many books he read, no book could ever bring him the peace of mind he sought and that all the research in the world would not satisfy his hungry heart. He had felt drawn to the caves for some time, where time itself did not exist. He felt pangs of guilt but knew that soul searching at the caves would ultimately bring him and the family much needed clarity.

Most caves happened to be occupied, but when he arrived, out of the darkness appeared a friendly face, beckoning him into her grotto. It was a woman about his own age, with a face he thought he knew, but could not quite pin down. She seemed to be swaddled in layers of linen which were a colourful mixture of earthy tones. Soon enough, he was handed a small tin of warm water with loose tea leaves swirling around, ladled from a large cooking bowl that hung over a firepit. The woman did not say a word but pointed to where he may lay himself down to rest, and soon enough he pulled out his blankets. He didn't notice the panther pendant slip out from his backpack but heard something jingle to the floor and thought nothing of it.

In the years that would follow, he would reflect how time itself in that brief period became irrelevant. Tim did not need 'time' to search, the answer came to him.

'For some it can take a lifetime and some never find the answer.'

The Christmas eve sunrise was exquisite and the colours on the rocks made the snow sparkle. Tim felt enlightened as he nestled under his blankets, watching the sunlight flood in, warming the rocks. Finding himself present and very much in the moment, something appeared at the mouth of the cave. An extremely large cat stood sideways, and shafts of light fought to break through and around it. It appeared wounded; its fur pecked at. Forlorn, it turned its head towards Tim, who instantly became enthralled in its gaze. It's eyes, just the right shade of blue, were mesmerizing, nourishing, and loving. Tim felt the urge to go over and console it, as much as he himself, felt the need to be consoled. Something began to glisten by the cat's front paw. Compelled to look, Tim stood up and as the blankets fell away, bending down, he saw what looked like a chain with a pendant attached. Picking it up, to his surprise it was a panther pendant just like Hannah's and looking up at the cat with the pendant in his hand, the realisation rushed over him that the large cat standing at the mouth of the cave was Parky the Panther. Tim felt a change come over him and Parky's wounds were instantly healed.

"I… I must go home. I wonder if this could be Hannah's. I must return it to her." Tim said stuttering, overwhelmed. "You are home now, my friend." Parky replied in his deep voice. "And yes, you should."

Without further instruction he packed his bag, bid the woman farewell, and headed home full of gratitude to be spending Christmas Eve with his family.

Meanwhile, Tom had also wandered up towards the higher ground in search of Tim and had come across the Flushing Waterfalls, driven by his instinct to go first to Pocklington, then up to the Falls and back through the caves. The Watcher clouds were prevalent on parts of his journey and just like Hannah, he felt intimidated by their beady eyes following his every move, but with renewed strength he resisted whatever doubt The Watchers were trying to feed him.

The falls had frozen in parts. Small icicles silently hung. Nearby, a couple of Watchers about the same age as Tom seemed to be suffering from 'Naution'. A type of nausea caused by the anxiety of visiting the falls or going through a cleansing process. Tom recognised the difficulty and temptations they were facing, having previously been in a similar situation himself and felt the need to encourage them to see the process through. Acknowledging him as a Gifted One, the two young men suddenly felt split loyalties and became fearful, knowing that the cleansing process was highly forbidden. Instead of trying to explain why they should proceed, Tom simply uttered to them, "I hope I am a good enough example of having been a Watcher, for you to proceed with the falls." They had heard of Tom and thanks to him they gained faith in their conversion, attracted The Great Stars attention, and the darkness simply fell away. Tom's witness had saved souls. He felt happy with himself as he walked off towards the caves and thought how finding Tim would make his day, plus impress Hannah. But there was no sign of him as Tom roamed around the rocks. Feeling his mission was in vain, his mood switched from high to low. It was at this point, having decided to head back to Hannah's, that he was accompanied by a man, perhaps slightly older than himself. At first, he felt wary as the man seemed to want to walk alongside him and chat about the going's on in Ashby-by-the-Sea. "Who do you think will win the final battle between The Watchers and The Gifted Ones?" The man asked. Tom was finding it hard to place him and feeling cold, found his chit chat irritating, yet at the same time, thought provoking. Then, the young man spoke in a deep profound voice and said, *"I guess the answer to it all is to simply keep believing."* Tom felt a warmth rush over him and as he glanced sideways, amazed in response to the man's statement, the man had disappeared and walking alongside him was Parky the Panther.

It was the greatest Gift of Christmas. When Tom returned to Hannah's, he felt elated with an incredible sense of worth. Tim was also excitedly sharing his journey with Belinda and the girls. He felt liberated. His mind, heart, eyes, and ears had all been opened, as he had freely accepted his Gift from The Great Star of the Cosmos. Tim presented the lost pendant to Hannah, and she leapt with joy. Amelia immediately confessed to her wrongdoing and instantly she was free from mental torment, having overcome the darkness. Belinda sat with Joy peacefully looking on, as the true gifts of Christmas were unfurled. It was a Christmas unlike any other. The Gifted in the Timms household, now all united, were more than ready for their meeting the next day with The Watchers.

Chapter Fifteen

Part One – Watchers Water Assault
Part Two – The Supper Battle

Watchers Water Assault

The Watchers were growing darker as The Gifted grew brighter.

As morning broke, the Timms garden was littered in black crow feathers, it was a stark contrast to the white snow and a perfect representation for what was occurring. Hannah was under no illusion of what lay ahead, having her confidence gain strength. She was resolute in continuing the journey, knowing that some of the battles had already been won.

It wasn't a visible enemy as such, as for much of the time the enemy were the hidden forces of evil, The Watchers, and their preying antics. She had a part to play once again, in this course of history. Her battle strategy, her humility towards Mr. Surlin, would hopefully burst the pride and arrogance of The Great Gifted Nickolous. What she was not yet aware of was the dishonourable intentions planned by The Watchers for a full-blown attack upon The Gifted, ahead of the pre-arranged evening meeting at the castle.

The feathers in the garden had been placed in a circular formation spreading out from the pond to the walls. Hannah peered out from her bedroom window at Queen Nail; Watcher clouds had consumed the sky almost covering the entire town. When she had looked, the eyes of the clouds seemed to pounce upon her. She had pulled back and in a surprising burst of anger, yanked the curtains shut, annoyed that The Watchers had breached the garden walls. Clearly irritated by the crow feathers in the garden, Queen Nail having read her mind, interceded to help, "Do not retaliate." She spoke. This intercession was occurring regularly and together they worked on positive ways to react to a potential attack, as well as Hannah's conduct, that evening at the castle.

Inside the house, Belinda had held a 'family' meeting and was now busy organising and steering her crew for what lay ahead. It was very similar to how Mini, and Hannah had prepared their imaginary friends during the summer. Her memory of Pentheus the leopard, reciting 'Stations, I say!' was an encouraging one. Everyone was going about preparing and honing their own imaginary friends' specific powers, ready for a potential battle with The Watchers, and the Timms just like Minis in the summer, became ablaze with light from their unfathomable capabilities.

Belinda could be seen petting Cork, having burst to life, jumping from his mount on the kitchen wall. She was trialling the best way to utilize his formidable antlers.

Amelia, feeling joyous once again but still very much 'Amelia,' was thoroughly enjoying bringing Joy to life, now for the right reasons. She was casting out Joy's thick long hair into nets and playing with the snake bracelets, in a way she hoped may aid The Gifted Ones. Tom was testing his unicorn's amazing ability to change size and colour. Tim, a keen newcomer to The Gifted world, looked upon it all in fascination. Spectating it all, Hannah's panther pendant glowed. She had missed it dearly in the brief time she had been without it.

In Ashby-by-the-Sea, many of infected Gifted Ones were now sitting prey at the castle, waiting to be terrorised by The Great Gifted Nickolous. For the fortunate ones unaffected, the Belief Council had issued a hand delivered card and it simply read, *'Believe and be on guard.'*

Hannah asked her dad if he would consider revisiting the caves and the Unsaids. She thought by sharing his newfound joy with them, some may be moved to support The Gifted Ones. Where once he would not have seen the logic in such a situation, he agreed and remained hopeful. Hannah had once again been directed by The Great Star and having listened, acted. The support The Gifted Ones would receive from Tim's visit to the caves was far different from what Hannah had originally intended, but having listened to The Star, she was the catalyst for greater things. So as a result, with time being of the essence, Tim set about returning to the caves. Once there, he met the same woman and after offering him tea, they both sat while she listened intently to him. When he mentioned his meeting with Parky the Panther she smiled warmly. She too was a Gifted One but had decided to remain living in seclusion at the caves. When she eventually did talk, she spoke in a tongue Tim did not recognise at first, but as she continued, remarkably, he found himself understanding! She spoke in the tongue of creatures and was a Gift bearer; a messenger from The Star. Tim, now a believer, became aware of his newfound unfathomable power instantly. Now, he would be able to freely converse with the animal kingdom; be it on land or sea, with creatures of all shapes and sizes, irrespective of his imagination.

The Gifted Ones had never been more ready.

As dusk fell, the tiny public address systems carried in the claws of The Watchercrows were flying over the town, relaying the recording of Mr. Surlin's message: *'My children, these waters run wild with the spirit of The Great Gifted Nickolous. I can assure you, one day these waters will rise and shower the shining.'*

It was a warning from The Watchers indicating that an assault would come in the air, in the form of water. With such a sorrowful event looming, the Watcher clouds had now blanketed the sky, suppressing the natural elements and filing the air with the distinct smell of algae.

The snow, distinguishing the season, was melting at speed and the air was becoming milder by the minute. A feeling of wetness was dampening the hearts and minds of the locals, killing their festive spirit. Something was occurring and fears were accumulating about the age-old rumours that existed about the castle.

Around late morning, the town fell exceedingly quiet, likened to the eeriness before a tsunami. One could hear a pin drop; a clock tick, any natural free flying birds were fleeing. It stopped the town in its tracks and throughout the entire area the ground began to shake. Up on the higher ground the caves trembled and the Gillaweep brook began bubbling uncontrollably, bursting its banks. In The Spinney, The Gifted neighbourhood, the homes were doing their best to remain strong, sturdy, and stable, but even they were incapable of sustaining such a phenomenon. For the older properties, like the Timms, the quake was causing serious devastation. Roof tiles flew like cards from a gamblers hand as they crashed to the ground. Windows cracked and inside many homes it was getting hard to move amidst the falling debris. The only unaffected buildings were the castle and the church. Following the quake, the Watcher clouds began to cry emptying themselves of their water, flooding the town and seeping into every nook and cranny. The storm continued to build with more trembles and more rain. It was about to reach its climax; the ground had shaken to its core and the clouds couldn't cry any more. Submerged deep underground, The Great Gifted Nickolous came slithering with gusto from out of the earth, bursting with anger out of the pond in the Timms garden, breaking the surrounding ground up to the walls and beyond.

His black coloured snake body, propelled upwards by his white wings, spiralled so high it seemed to touch the Watcher clouds. Reaching dizzying heights, he then summoned The Watchers, hissing aloud, saying, *"RISSSSSSE my children and shower the shining!"*

As he soared into the sky, the waters in and around the town erupted, walls of water from the brook and falls rose, with the likeness and power of geysers. Flying Watcherfish of all sizes were thrust upwards, leaping from out of the waters. Some immense, the size of a house, ready to seek out The Gifted Ones unfathomable powers by emitting their grey force and crushing their imaginative powers. The multitude of Watcherfish, with their bodies of a lizard and face and beak of a crow, made the sky look prehistoric, casting large shadows below. What seemed like endless numbers of Watcherfish were unleashed, flying out of the huge columns of waters and from the skies bombing down darting in between the waters, came the Watchercrows. The waters rose until they could rise no more and following a deadly pause they crashed down to the ground. It was as though a plug had been pulled from the sky. The water spilt everywhere, swamping the town, resulting in damage that was inconceivable.

The Great Gifted Nickolous dropped back into the pond, leaving his faithful behind to pillage The Gifted. Sadly, as in most conflicts, the innocent ones were instantly caught up in the battle. Plumes of grey light emitted from The Watchers was ripping through the air, targeting any living thing. Don Surlin, the largest of the gigantic Watcherfish, led the attack, followed closely by eleven others in close formation, varying in sizes. Their size reflected their power force, and each wore a chain with a pendant in the image of The Great Gifted Nickolous – a winged snake with the beak and face of a crow.

Ashby-by-the-Sea was in bedlam. Strobes of strong grey light were being emitted from every Watcher. The image, as they expelled their power, could have been likened to the light from a spaceship, in a sci-fi film. Their force jabbed intermittently like pellets from a machine gun, Naturals were running for their lives, not understanding the 'unnatural' phenomena taking place, whilst The Gifted were falling to the ground and their imaginary friends obliterated.

The snake from Mr. Surlin's store sign, slithered up the shop's facade reaching the top. It then continued to slink its way across the rooftops, looking for cracks to enter, in the hope of encountering a Gifted One. As soon as this snake had found an opportunity to attack, another snake broke from the sign and so it continued, these were protégé's of The Great Gifted Nickolous. Absent of white wings, but with the same face and beak of a crow, these serpents were the silent killers that sought out to destroy the Gifted Ones light.

The Timms, although initially stunned, like all The Gifted, were ready. Each went about their mission independently in defence of The Gifted Ones, safe in the knowledge that Parky and The Great Star were always with them. The garden had been destroyed in the attack and the statue of Queen Nail lay on its side having toppled off the steps. Seeing her, Hannah fleetingly panicked, thinking that her Gift would not be able to bring her to life and that she was broken, but of course her Gift was not of this world and with their spiritual unity, a power was formed that far exceeded any external decay. The Gifted's power was blossoming, better and brighter than ever before. Hannah's panther pendant had gained mini wings, reminiscent to the panther fairies from Mini's portrait and as the pendant pulsated, the wings gently flapped, and the light beamed out from Hannah's chest.

Watchercrows perched arrogantly on parts of the crumbled garden wall, but seeing Queen Nail from Hannah's power, they cowardly fled. They knew the intensity of their combined power, putting their own in jeopardy, even though the reward for capturing the panther was huge.

Parky's spirit had planted a thought in Hannah's mind, to attend to the Watchers whose Gifts could be redeemed. Queen Nail nodded to Hannah casting the 'Armour of Light' around them as they were transformed into mermaids and headed straight over to Pocklington. Both very much Queen's, but one without a crown, were brilliant in their battle armour of belief, and dazzled in their attire. Queen Nail in her royal blue ensemble with her crown of stars, whilst Hannah shone in every shade of white imaginable. With the brook waters in disarray, they moved in the same motion through the air, as if in water. It was absurd really, heading to the home of enemy territory, but Queen Nail knew that The Watchers who stayed behind were the ones worth redeeming, unsure of their role in the battle. The scene was not that different to when Hannah had first visited Pocklington; they arrived by Mrs. Robinson's cottage. Having the same sad look on her face, she was nervously calling the same young Watcher boys, clearly wanting to keep them out of trouble and under the radar. The boys were happily playing in the decimation of the brook and naughtily they ignored her plea. Seeing her look turn to that of desperation, Queen Nail stepped in, restoring her belief. "Stay still dear." She said to Hannah, casting the armour of light far and wide to cover the boys and Mrs. Robinson. The boys, sensing something had changed, instinctively ran towards Mrs. Robinson who was wearing her long skirt. She placed a hand on each of their heads and then looking at Queen Nail, a tiny smile appeared. She was not at all alarmed by her presence or that of Hannah's and a feeling of relief washed over her.

"Even in sad times, there is still much love to give and receive," Queen Nail said. *"But only if you believe, and now, is the time."* Mrs. Robinson's nod was the yes for Queen Nail to proceed, saying, *"Now, imagine all kind of wonderful things,"* First she looked to the boys, who were in complete acceptance of their unusual visitor's presence. Then to Mrs. Robinson, "You too, Mrs. Robinson."

As the three Watchers began to imagine, the light radiating from their chests reflected their intentions to be free and cleansed from the darkness. Queen Nail laid her hands upon each of them, her nails turning from blue to dazzling white, restoring their Gift. It was not hard for the boys to be restored or Mrs. Robinson; she was ready.

Queen Nail and Hannah went on to save many more souls, before ushering them to a safe place. But this was only part of the battle, Hannah's exemplary imaginary friend, Queen Nail, would need to use her nails to defend as they headed into the eye of the storm with all eyes on the ultimate prize, the panther pendant.

As they moved by the castle, on their way to Market Street, The Watchers encroached their space, drawn to their overwhelming energies, and emitting dark forces. It was then Queen Nail put up her defence. Using her nails to shield Hannah's imaginary Gift, with Hannah by her side, she raised her hands whilst facing the enemy all around them. Then with flat palms, as much to say 'STOP,' some of them instantly fled. To those still standing, she turned her palms over and built a barrier to obstruct their power. With her fingers spread wide, each nail gained the strength of steel, turning a dazzling white, this time to blind the enemy. Like moths to a flame, Flying Watcherfish and Watchercrows flew into the bright light, only to be stunned by the shield, and dazed by the light.

With the unrelenting rain from the Watcher clouds, the barrage of Watchers was unforgiving. Hannah was thankful to see other Gifted Ones, including her own family, take the brunt.

High upon the rooftops the rain was pounding the tiles, before smacking to the ground and standing sturdy up on the ridge, was Cork with Belinda. A stag of unfathomable superiority, his razor-sharp antlers spanned the skyline. Hannah could hear her mother's husky tones as they battled the snakes from the chemist. In one fell swoop Cork mercilessly sliced or speared them; in Belinda's imagination he was made for this moment and bore the sword of the Spirit. Like an outraged cowgirl, she swung her leg over his back, he snorted, and together they flew. His mighty antlers acted as wings, whilst still piercing through oncoming Flying Watcherfish and crows.

Hannah looked on in pride, as her mother and her beloved stag moved onto saving more Gifted Ones, by destroying any uncertainty and retaining their belief. Cork's antlers pierced through any forces of doubt from The Watchers; his penetrating gaze was truly formidable. With his intermittent cough, he reminded her of both Pentheus and Parky. It seemed all The Gifted Ones imaginary friends were different but held similarities. Perhaps it was a culmination of the fruit of The Star.

Back in the Timm's home, like a true matriarch, Mini held fort. Hannah's dream had foretold the attack that was about to take place. Tiny Flying Watcherfish were now flying from out of the Cuckoo Clock into the house. Somehow, someway, they had managed to invade and were gaining numbers at speed. In no time, Mini's magic and unfathomable powers rectified the situation and retorting, tiny, winged panthers flew from out of the light pouring down from her portrait. Tiny, yet mighty, the panther wings batted The Watchers out of existence, with their unparalleled presence and panther power velocity.

Amelia flicked her hair confidently, having bought Joy to life. They were fighting off The Watchers in The Spinney, feeling an affinity towards the Gifted, who like herself, had been cruelly taken advantage of. The Watchers had manipulated many here, by casting doubt in their minds. Joy's thick long silky hair wove into large nets, which cast into what seemed like an infinite amount of space, to catch Watchercrows or Flying Watcherfish. Having netted them, she then hurled her hair like a supersonic shot putter, casting them into oblivion, disposing of her catch with a high-pitched giggle.

Tim ruffled his wet hair, keeping a low profile as he trudged through the water in town. He found himself surprised at how 'unsurprised' he now felt, as the astonishing unfathomable events were unfolding. Happy his family were at work and comfortable they were safe under the protection of The Star, he was now waiting for an opportunity to serve the Gifted himself and use his wonderous new power of talking in tongues with the animal kingdom. It came almost straight away, sadly in the form of creatures who had become victims of the battle. Outside the Bakery, Ben & Dale were taking injured animals into the back of their shop, as discreetly as possible. Many birds, dogs, and cats as well as numerous other creatures had been injured, hit by either falling debris or from the crashing waters, and were floating helplessly in the flooded streets and gutters. "Can I help?" Tim said crouching over, as Bob gently picked up yet another dog from the gutter before wrapping a blanket over him. "Sure, thank you Tim, but the problem is we are incapable of treating them, so we will just show them love and kindness, I guess."

"Maybe that's where I can help." Tim replied warmly. Bob raised his eyebrows, thinking his talents went beyond science and as we know, now they did.

The water had seeped onto the shop floor, but in the back stood several large trolleys with numerous shelves, used for storing bread, this was where the injured lay. "At least they're out of the wet." Ben said gently, showing Tim. Looking over each trolley, Tim got himself acquainted with the different species and slowly, one by one, he began to hear them talk. "It's my right wing that's the bother." Said a small sparrow on the top shelf. "Well, it's my leg." Said a dog on a lower shelf. "I am cut." Whined a black cat. Then another, and another, all describing their aliments.

Tim was amazed and enthralled, partaking in as many conversations and helping where he could. Little did he know that he was not only serving The Great Star's divine creation, but also himself becoming a Gift bearer, because as the animals spoke, Ben and Dale both noticed how they too were also able to understand. Both men were on the verge of discovering that they bore the same Gift as Tim, and in that moment, their hearts were opened. All they would need to do from now on was to believe. *For only if they truly believed would they be able to use their miraculous powers.* Hugging one another, Tim felt blessed to be granted friends that had a similar Gifted power to him, especially so soon after receiving his.

Overall, The Gifted were triumphing and Victor, as protector of The Gifted, was working hard creating diversions whilst staying under The Watchers radar; it was hard for him.

Mr. and Mrs. Cox, now free from their own mental torture, were ushering the vulnerable into 'The Star of the Sea' church crypt. Hannah had intuitively called it the 'Safe Place' when she flew over it with Parky and now it was. Mrs. Robinson and the boys and many other saved souls were already there, bravely brought in by Hannah and Queen Nail. Mrs. Cox was back in her element, being a 'bright busy body', running her own 'air raid' type storm shelter.

The Gifted were pulling together in many ways. At the Butchers, Mr. & Mrs. Harrison had created their own shelter. The heavy doors fitted with weather strips not only kept out unwanted beastly micro-Watchers, but also kept much of the water at bay. As soon as trouble arose, Mr. Harrison had bravely bellowed into the street, 'Come! Take refuge here!' and Mrs. Harrison was now making copious amounts of tea with the emergency hot water they had. Even Bob the postman was safe, for now.

Hannah was blown away when she saw Tom sweep by on his unicorn, as valiant as before, in the Battle of Minds. Except this time, he seemed braver, more mature, more handsome. All these feelings made her flush momentarily and the same sensation she had experienced before returned, the dancing of butterflies in her tummy, proving her love for him. Tom's unfathomable power was most dramatic, as he approached Mr. Surlin and the other gigantic Flying Watcherfish. His Gift enabled his unicorn to change size, from tiny, black in colour, to colossal and dazzling white. As at Mini's in the summer, the unicorn overshadowing the enemy, batted away Watchers into obscurity. Hannah looked up into the sky, he looked like a Greek God astride a mythical creature, and she blushed again.

Mr. Surlin, clearly intimidated, began to summon The Watchers, and retreat. He knew they were losing control of the situation. Hannah saw Beth and Rene fly by as they too retreated. It was strange she thought how she still recognised them, even though they were transformed into Watcherfish. "Tonight, is the night" they taunted, whilst wildly flapping their wings. "BYE-BYE PARKY THE PANTHER" they shouted, as they flew by.

Part two – The Supper Battle

The Watchers had withdrawn for now and Hannah with the rest of the family were gathered at home, which had been damaged during the battle. For many of The Gifted, their valued contribution had now concluded, but for Hannah it was only the warmup act, and it was Mini she desired to talk with the most. There was still time thankfully, to regroup and refresh ahead of the meeting at the castle. Everyone, except Hannah, was in the kitchen and much was being discussed about the day's events so far, along with what may, or may not happen that evening.

The Watcher clouds had also retreated, but remnants of raindrops still clung to Hannah's bedroom window as she stared apprehensively out. One perfectly formed raindrop bore a tiny reflection and Hannah knelt up on her bed towards the window, to take a closer look. It stood out from the others and having gained gravity was slipping down the pane. It seemed to stick to the window like a tiny oval shaped looking glass, within it a bright light appeared with pointed ends, in the shape of a tiny star. Minute in size, yet accurate in detail, she recognised it as The Great Star of The Cosmos. It felt wonderful to look at it and the more she gazed, the more sublime she felt, and her pendant pulsated and glowed. However, Belinda downstairs had been calling Hannah a few times, beckoning her to join them in the kitchen. Whilst she really didn't want to be distracted from what she felt was a state of bliss, she nevertheless left her room to descend downstairs. As before, her mother had acted intuitively to a greater plan, as Hannah reached the bottom of the stairs, a shaft of light from Mini's portrait cast over the bottom part of the stairs. Clearly Mini had a desire to talk as well.

"Mini!" Hannah said, as her grandmother appeared. She was always so happy to see her.

"Your time has nearly arrived, darling. The Gifted life, as you know in many ways, is a battle of the mind. But remain open to receiving an even greater gift. *To believe more, we need to believe more.* The reign of The Gifted is at hand, no frills needed. The Watchers let frills become a way of necessity. When we, The Gifted, give our body, mind, and heart, we give our all. There is no room for extras, no comforts." Hannah listened intently; she always did. Mini spoke in a profound manner, just as she had in the summer. "And lastly, do not be afraid. There is nothing to be afraid of." As she spoke, a tear came to her eye. It reminded Hannah of the tear on the windowsill. *'A tear so bright, it shone full of hope, full of love.'*

"Thank-you Mini. Always together in heart. I love you."

"And I love you too darling. More than you can ever imagine." She replied winking.

Dusk crept in, darkening the doors of The Gifted. The children of light were not daunted, and Tim had found several hand-held flame torches in the attic room, to carry in their procession to the castle. "Oh Tim, good idea. We want to shine bright, don't we girls!" Belinda said rallying the crew. Each of The Gifted played their part, with Belinda performing her role consistently.

Tim, Belinda, Amelia, and Tom had agreed to join Hannah at the meeting with Mr. Surlin. Ann from the Belief Council, accompanied by Mrs. Gives to physically aid her, had also confirmed they would be attending. It was agreed that upon arrival they would *not* be escorted visibly, by their imaginary friends. *"True friends walk alongside us even when they are not visibly there."* Ann had said to Hannah during the day, whilst defending The Gifted. She was so happy to know that all had worked out well in the Timms household. Her insight was indeed a great Gift but not even Ann had the foresight of The Star.

The torches' flames burnt through the damp air as they walked, without really planning it, in the following formation:

Hannah at the front, followed by:

Amelia & Tom

Ann, on the arm of Mrs. Gives

Belinda & Tim

Belinda and Tim each carried a basket in one hand, as suggested by Ann, with ample food and drink in each. The smell of algae was now rather overbearing. Belinda had somehow quickly made-up snoods for everyone to slip over their faces, at least until they arrived at the castle, to help with the overbearing aroma. She was slightly annoyed with herself that she had not thought or organised these before.

It was the day after Christmas day and a few minutes before 11pm. The Gifted, dressed each in their own individual style, arrived upon the castles higher ground by the huge tower with its imposing battlements. Slowly, and staying tightly together with their torches, they walked amongst the ruins. Some Watchercrows had registered their arrival and a series of deafening squawks followed. The moon shone through the large empty arched windows, casting shadows.

It was in this area, in what would have originally been the great hall of the castle, that the captured Gifted Ones were kept. They were lined up against a huge stone wall standing silently and the light from the torches revealed the petrified look on their faces. Everyone was shocked and deeply saddened to see their fellow Gifted Ones in this state. Knowing that some of them had been held there for some time was extremely upsetting. Hannah gave them all a tight reassuring smile, but they returned her gesture with a dazed look, some just dropped their heads down. Taking a deep breath to steady her thoughts she peered up into the sky and noticed it had completely cleared, with the pure moonlight the sky was littered with more stars than could ever be imagined.

High on one of the walls, near to where they were all gathered, about halfway up, was the ruin of what would have been an open fireplace, in a large upper room. Many Flying Watcherfish were flapping around it. So, they decided that here they should lay down the baskets they had bought on the ground below it.

Mr. Surlin with his entourage of nine arrived as Watchercrows flying down in front of the fireplace. They took a cursory glance pecking at The Gifted Ones basket, before walking out of their dark alter egos. "SOOO, we meet again." Mr. Surlin said in his creepy way, standing near to Hannah, staring at her pendant. A tiny snake slithered across the iris of his eye, disappearing through his pupil. "Quite a show you put on today." He remarked.

Hannah overlooked the battle talk. She was not here to discuss tactics, strategies or who had the better army. She was here to resolve the ongoing dispute. "Mr. Surlin, before we talk, can you please release The Gifted Ones you hold captive here."

"We are hoping you will *all* be released from the delusional world *you* live in Hannah. There are some of you with such *great* potential!" His tone was as slippery as the snake that donned the chain around his neck. He was looking directly towards Amelia and Tom. "Let me show you what happens to those who do not obey."

From the crowd of Watchers that had gathered, he summoned over two young men. Tom thought they looked like the young men from the falls, but he wasn't sure. Then, he publicly humiliated them. "Betrayal comes at a high price and The Great Gifted Nickolous does not take kindly to it." His potent, powerful grey power force hit the young men, transforming them permanently into Watchercrows. They shamefully flew off, back to their new home on castle Walk, with the other Watchercrows. The Gifted knew of this form of punishment and looked on in absolute horror, particularly Tom.

The meeting was not going as they had hoped, the intensity had increased further, when rising from over the castle wall appeared the monster himself, The Great Gifted Nickolous. Many of The Watchers lowered their heads in respect, as they had in the council chamber. He was of gargantuan proportion, so it didn't take him long to slither down the wall and reaching the ground he faced Don Surlin hissing, "S s s s s Surlin, your work is done here."

"Yes master." He replied, lowering his head until it almost touched the ground in reverence. Don Surlin, the leader of the Spectacle Council, took tiny steps back in a lowly fashion.

The Great Gifted Nickolous swayed over to The Gifted Ones. Hannah was still standing at the helm. Rising slightly in front of her, he said, "You do know that it was I, yes I, that terrified your grandfather to death; he betrayed your grandmother!"

Hunter Lang, Mini's husband, Belinda's father and grandfather to Amelia and Hannah, had tried desperately hard to resist The Watchers temptations when he had moved from America with Mini to Ashby-by-the-Sea. He frequented the flushing meadows and falls often, but his ambitious nature was a contributing factor which led to his demise. He had accepted a bribe to keep 'Watch' on the future of his wonderful, Gifted family, Mini was pregnant at the time. After much reflection and confiding in Mini, he had decided to cast the money away, over the crypt of The Great Gifted Nickolous. Unbeknown, the evil master was waiting to terrorise him to death.

The image of her grandfather flashed before her, dead in the castle grounds, lying flat, face upwards, with a petrified look on his face. The Great Gifted Nickolous was succeeding, looking for a hook, seeing her sorrowful face. "I will do the same to you if you do not surrender. You *will* be my Queen Hannah, with the panther at your side, for eternity."

Calmly, Ann left the formation and unaided walked around in front of Hannah, her dog following behind and together they faced the beast. Her 'Believe' necklace shone brilliantly.

Nickolous laughed with a hissing sound at her bravery and slowly stooped to Ann's height, then like lightening, reared up and darted down in front of the dog. Jabbing the poor defenceless hound, in rapid movements, before sticking its tongue out hissing, it created the most fearful face ever to be seen. The dog's ears pricked up and flopped on its side, killed by the sheer terror. Ann's blindness had saved her, but The Great Gifted Nickolous was not done as he projected his lethal power force, grey in colour with deadly black streaks, upon her.

Suddenly, from the side, and in everyone's peripheral vision, something flew into the force, trying to block it. It was Victor. He stared boldly back at the master who he thought he once loved and admired and who he had exonerated from his evilness. Victor was ready to pay the ultimate sacrifice and die for his true friends, his family, The Gifted Ones. The force, so powerful, caused his crow body to explode into dust, and the few feathers that remained, swirled, floating to the ground, followed by his chain. As Ann fell helplessly to the ground, what seemed to look like star dust began to rise from her chest, forming a constellation in the outline of her body, shinning in the clear night sky.

The combination of Victor's death, believed to be a faithful servant, together with Ann's victory caused The Great Gifted Nickolous to give out an almighty, deafening squawk, combined with a hiss. Outraged, the ground began to rumble, and the castle shook. Finding it hard to keep their balance, The Gifted were unable to attend to Ann's body. Out of the body of The Great Gifted Nickolous broke more snake proteges. The sight was both horrifying and sickening. In defence, The Gifted Ones brought their imaginary friends to life, but it was too late. His poisonous force flew to the favoured Gifted One, striking Hannah, tossing her body, shaking it violently until she hit the ground. Everything stopped. It was as though the world had gone silent and time stood still. The quake stopped and not a sound could be heard as Hannah lay motionless. The Great Gifted Nickolous was moments away from retrieving the pendant. In the few yards between them, he shrewdly extended his beak towards her chain, to snatch the pendant away, however it was still glowing and pulsating greater than ever before, and distracted ahead, in his midst stood an even greater presence. Parky the panther. Walking stealthily in a majestic manner, with eyes composed, up behind The Gifted Ones, he approached Hannah.

Some of the onlooking Watchers fell to their knees, belief in their Gift restored, whilst others retreated. The Great Gifted Nickolous, spineless in every possible way, pulled back, fleeing from sight. Parky sniffed then nuzzled Hannah's entire body, the strength of his head made her topple then flop back. Then in silence, he sat poised without a word, as though he was keeping guard.

The Gifted Ones with their imaginary friends gathered around. Belinda, propped up by Tim, collapsed down to her knees by Hannah's side, holding her tiny limp hand. "Tim, I think she's dead." Tim stood dazed with his hands in his hair. Amelia burst into uncontrollable tears, and Tom, in shock, robotically put his arm around her. Mrs. Gives went over to attend to Ann's body close by.

A vastness of space seemed to surround The Gifted, distancing them from the few remaining Watchers. In the night sky The Great Star of the Cosmos appeared, its long rays seemed to shine upon the space below, and from The Star came a voice. A voice so loud yet so peaceful that it would have been impossible not to hear or feel its reverberation,

"You can kill the flesh but not the spirit. Hannah is only sleeping. Rise, little one."

One of the stars rays touched Hannah's foot, and from her body she rose, in an ethereal way. She went over to each member of her family, including Tom and consoled them, whilst Parky spoke.

"The Gifted journey continues, and the victory of this battle has once again, been life over death. Hannah will join me in spirit because The Watchers are not defeated. They still exist. In many ways her mission has only begun. Safe with me, she will voyage through time, to the beginning. Together, the light will overcome the darkness."

As he spoke the weather began to change. The clear sky had created a crispness in the air and shining particles began to sprinkle from the heavens. Translucent snowflakes fell all around but did not settle on the ground.

Hannah turned to Parky and mounting his back, together upon the ray, they ascended in spirit to The Great Star. Turning her head, she looked back and smiled at her earth family. They watched her go, and her body, asleep for now, turned into dust, and was absorbed into the flakes that fell.

The Star all night long, hung over the castle like a huge prehistoric albatross, and we all know that an albatross is a good omen. The Gifted in Ashby-by-the-Sea were free from evil for now and the family lived in hope to be reunited with Hannah again someday.

For it is in trust that we go forward, to believe. And I, the Great Star of the Cosmos, shall continue to share The Panther Tales, taking you back to when it all began.

In the beginning.

For where there is good there is always evil.

THE END

Daniella Marie Rushton is British, born 1973.

Wife to Nicholas and Mother to Bertie.

In 2017, her son challenged her to channel her renowned imagination into writing a book. The Panther Tales fantasy series was born.

'The Watchers and the Gifted Ones' book one in the series, published in 2020.

'The Queen and the Powerful Pendant' the sequel, published in 2022

She has since gone onto collate a collection of fairy tales, of which one has been published online, as well as a collection of surreal poetry, which she hopes to have published someday soon.

Her brand, 'Fantasy, Fairy Tales and Poetry' has developed, inspired by her Christian faith, as well as living a thoroughly creative life. This belief, the core message of The Panther Tales, has led to her being featured on numerous podcasts, radio, as well as summits discussing and sharing her literary life journey.

Follow a winged panther and Daniella on:

Instagram, Facebook, and Twitter

@thepanthertales

www.thepanthertales.com

Printed in Great Britain
by Amazon